I0847355

ISBN: 979-8-9900569-3-0

©2025
Published in the United States of America
All Rights Reserved

Cover image by Wanlop Pinyowong via iStock Photo

Book Design & Editing Assistance by Pink Eraser Press

One Good Thing

Kate Kaminski

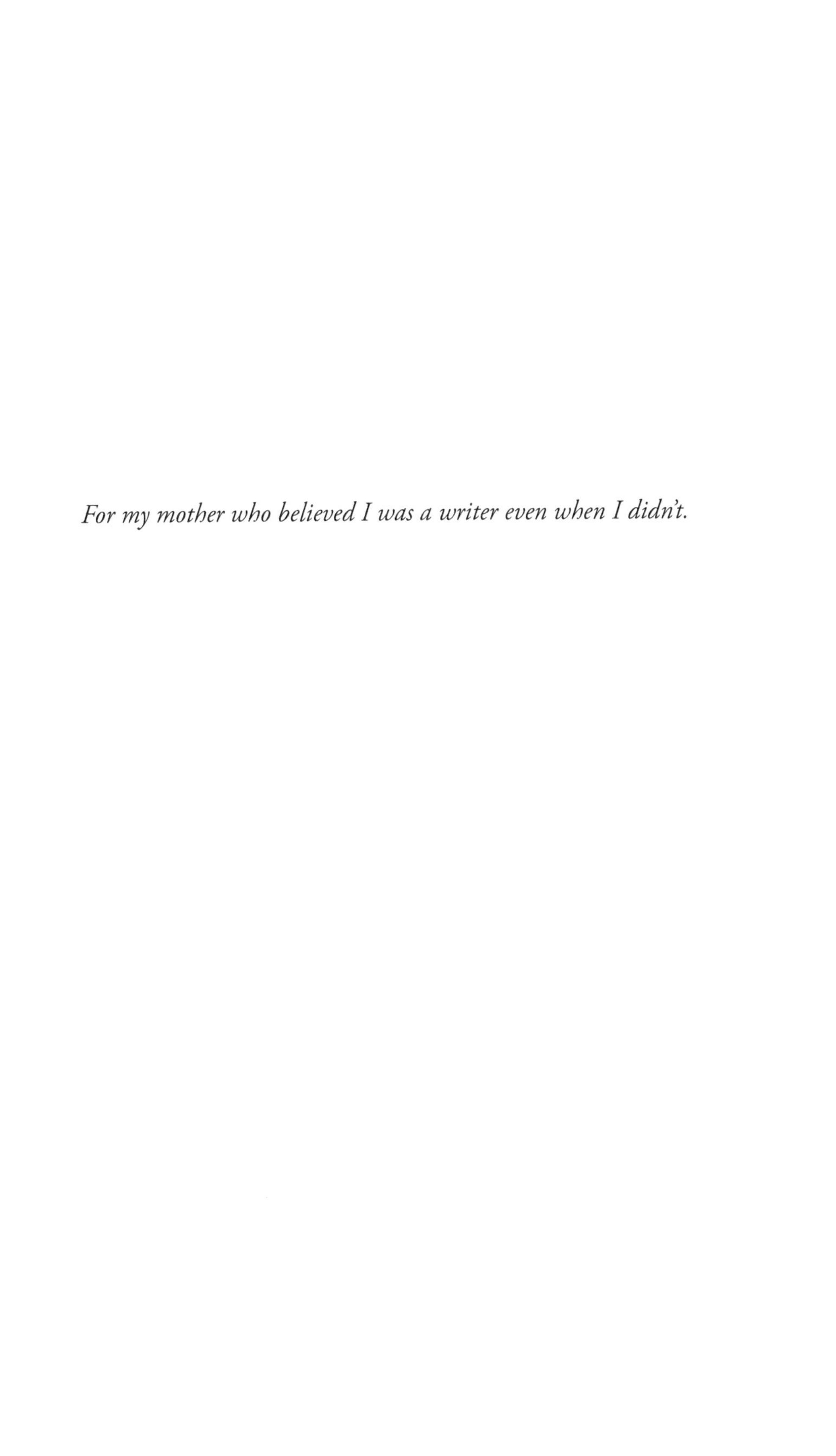

For my mother who believed I was a writer even when I didn't.

Chapter 1

Kiki, 1992

On the second to last day of her vacation, Kiki decides that Niagara Falls was a bad idea. The man lying in the heart-shaped bed snores in his sleep. They were both so drunk, nothing happened, but the memory of his fumbling, bumbling touching makes her feel even more lonely at five in the morning when nothing is stirring. Even the falls seem to have gone silent and reproachful.

She wonders if she should just check out and leave him there, go stay somewhere else her last night, somewhere without heart-shaped beds and red velvet ball fringe on the bedspread, somewhere she won't be reminded that no matter how much she wishes it weren't true, she is alone and will always be alone.

But what about Schmuck? Doesn't he count? At least he's somebody. He'll be up by now, even if he'd also spent the previous night drinking (which, in all likelihood, he had). She could call him, and he would talk to her, ask her how her vacation was going, tell her he missed her and to hurry home, tell her how much he needed her. But maybe he would be grumpy, hungover, monosyllabic and eager to get off the phone. Either scenario was possible with Schmuck.

The man stirs, rolls over, groaning. He will have a doozy of a hangover when he finally decides to open his eyes. On the way back from the bar (walking, of course!), he'd stopped at the 24-hour liquor store and bought a pint of Jim Beam and a pint of Jägermeister, both of which they had polished off, trading shot for shot until they both passed out. Kiki has already had two cups of bad coffee and three ibuprofens, her standard formula for staving off whatever regrets she might otherwise have about what she'd done the night before.

If somebody had asked her, why take her one week of vacation on the New York side of Niagara Falls, Kiki would have been hard-pressed to give a truthful answer because the truth was too ugly to be spoken. She might have said that the place represents romance and she hoped to meet somebody, fall in love and never return to Pennsylvania, even if that let Schmuck down because he relies on her so much. She might have claimed that she'd always been fascinated by the awesome power of the falls or that her favorite movie was *Niagara* starring Marilyn Monroe in one of her finest dramatic performances. But the truth was something far less straightforward and a lot darker. It was the idea, like a persistent, quiet hum, that by coming here she might decide to throw herself into those roiling waters and permanently escape from who she still is.

You can't run away from who you are because you only find yourself at the finish line.

She'd read that in some book a long time ago, and it was depressingly true. And six days in, Kiki has avoided the main attraction, has ignored that humming (drowned it with booze), at least for the moment. Didn't that prove she wasn't ready? That there is still hope for her?

The man rolls over again with a small moan, and Kiki sees that he has an erection. What must he be dreaming about? She grimaces. It's the sign she needs and, as quickly and quietly as she can, she packs her bag, grabs her toothbrush and toiletries and sneaks out of the room while he sleeps on. She hangs the tag on the door that invites the maid to make up the room, picturing the man being rudely awakened and finding her gone, gone, gone.

In the parking lot, she throws her bag in the back and drives down the road about a mile to a Holiday Inn, asking for a room on the back side, facing away from the falls. That option has dissipated into the constant mist generated by the thundering waters, and she's sick of thinking about it.

Schmuck answers on the tenth ring, sounding slightly out of breath but happy that it's her. She tells him she'll be home the following day and the old man does tell her how much he misses her, but Kiki knows he's probably thinking about how when she's away, he can do what he pleases and drink all day if he wants to, sitting alone in his stuffy office. She doesn't judge though. He's given her too much for no reason other than the goodness of his pickled heart.

When she hangs up, the day yawns, empty, in front of her. The sun is hidden behind storm-gray clouds. Since it's a Thursday, the commercial strip where her hotel is located is busy with weekday traffic. Kiki can't go back to the same all-day bar where she met the man. Besides, she doesn't really feel like drinking. So she asks the front desk where to find the mall. Shopping is always a good distraction.

Chapter 2

1992

"How about lunch at Chuck E. Cheese?" Leona asks, holding Janet by the hand and hustling her through the school parking lot.

Janet is still crying quietly, tears dripping off the end of her nose.

"You can wear your tutu."

Janet side-eyes Leona, gauging her mother's sincerity. She wipes at the snot oozing from her short little nose with the back of her hand and stumbles a little.

Leona's patience is waning. "Stop crying, Janet."

Janet sniffles.

"They didn't hurt you. You're fine."

"They did!" She stops, pulls up her shirt to show Leona a flat, inch-wide, raised red bump across the front of her chubby abdomen.

Leona looks at it critically. "You'll be fine." She sets off toward their cherry-red Toyota parked in the red-lined, restricted zone.

"It hurts," sniffles Janet to herself.

She follows Leona. There's no point in arguing with her mother when she's decided what Janet is feeling.

In the car, Janet says about the two little boys who cornered her on the playground, "I hate them."

Distracted by the heavy traffic, Leona is focused on turning left, her head swiveling right, then left, then right again. She guns it just ahead of a large pickup truck who then tailgates her for the next mile.

Janet says again, "I hate them."

"You don't hate them. You shouldn't hate people."

"They hate *me*," Janet says. "They *hit* me! With *books*!"

"They'll be punished."

"Mrs. Corelli hates me too."

Leona heaves a sigh. "Please, Janet. Try not to focus on the negative shit."

"Shit," Janet says.

Leona laughs. "That's my girl."

At home, Janet trudges upstairs to put on her orange "tutu," which is actually a double-flounced slip that used to be Leona's. Leona has altered it into a kind of ballet costume for Janet after wearing it to a party where the good-looking cousin of her boss's wife tore it while they were making out in the garage. After he'd torn it, she'd shoved him, and then he'd called her a tease, and after that, she hadn't been invited back. Which was fine. But if she's honest, she really kind of hates that orange tutu.

Leona locates the Chuck E. Cheese two-for-one coupon and calls up the stairs, "Hurry up!"

Janet appears at the top landing. "Can I wear my ballet shoes, too?"

Leona is disappointed (but not surprised) to find the restaurant packed, even on a weekday. They park miles away from the entrance, and gripping Janet firmly by the hand, Leona bobs and weaves her way through the parking lot to get to the door before the other, less efficient parents and children.

Inside Leona pushes past and snags a four-top booth ahead of a man with three boys, flashing the scowling dad a triumphant smile.

Janet says, "Can we get French fries too?"

Leona frowns. "You're not *that* injured."

Leona wishes Janet would eat faster. She's bored and getting irritated by the clamor of all these children. She looks across the table at Janet, who takes tiny bites along the ragged edge of a slice of pizza, then chews thoughtfully, cow-like. She swings her legs, and each time the square wooden toe of her ballet shoe scrapes the floor, it makes this annoying squeak.

Sometimes Leona wishes Janet were...different. Sometimes she thinks, *this child is nothing like me.* And: *why is she like this?* If two older boys had tried to bully her at Janet's age, she'd have given them a knuckle sandwich or died trying. But apparently, Janet hadn't fought back at all, had just let them abuse her. Such a passive child. A natural victim. It worries Leona. It really does. It worries her almost as much as it annoys her.

"Janet," Leona says, "can you stop doing that with your feet, please? It's giving me a headache."

Janet stops chewing, goes still. "Sorry, Mommy." Then she swallows and places the pizza crust on top of a pile of discarded pizza crusts. Neither of them eats the crusts because Leona says that's where all the calories are.

"Mommy, I don't feel good," Janet says and, immediately after, vomits forcefully into her token cup, which the spew quickly overflows, spilling onto her tutued lap.

Leona bullets out of her seat, hand over mouth, and rushes away toward the bathroom.

"Ew, Dad! That's gross!"

Janet turns her head. The boys and their scowling father are staring at her. She can't move. She burps, gags, the acrid smell of the vomit burning her nose.

The man hurries his kids into their coats and pushes them toward the door, leaving their half-eaten pizza. Nobody else seems to have noticed because Janet looks around and everybody's eating like nothing's happened. She looks down at her lap and starts to cry.

Leona bursts through the restroom door and bolts to the first sink, leaning over and resting her elbows on the countertop.

"Oh god, oh god, oh god," she says, fighting her gag reflex, swallowing convulsively. A second or two and it passes. She looks up.

A well-dressed woman is standing at the next sink over, washing her hands. They exchange glances in the mirror: Leona offering a lopsided smile, the woman's eyes gliding over Leona without warmth.

"Hey, sorry about that," Leona says, waving her hand vaguely.

The woman nods.

"My little girl just threw up out there." Leona laughs, a harsh sound. "That's how *my* day's going."

The woman is carefully rinsing her hands, apparently uninterested, which is pretty irritating.

"My little girl, Janet? She just threw up her whole damn lunch. She's eight and has a sensitive stomach. But she does love pizza."

The snooty woman reaches for paper towels.

"Can't handle vomit, know what I mean? Shit I can handle. When she was two, she used to eat her boogers. That was hard. But vomit? No way."

The woman crumples and tosses the paper towels, then reaches into her neat shoulder bag and withdraws a comb, runs it through her perfectly smooth, chin-length, light brown hair.

"Figure if I wait in here, somebody else will—you know—take care of it.

So I don't have to."

The woman drops the comb into her purse, snaps it shut, adjusts it on her shoulder.

"You don't have a cigarette, do you?" Leona asks.

The woman smiles faintly, as if to herself, then turns and goes out.

"Wow. Fuck you, too," Leona says.

She turns on the tap and splashes water on her cheeks.

The woman threads her way through the mobs of screaming children and harried parents. She's looking for somebody.

There. The chubby little girl in the ill-fitting dress layered with a raggedy makeshift tutu, holding a cup in her hand filled with foul-smelling vomit.

"Janet?"

Janet looks up, frowns.

"You're Janet."

Janet nods.

"Come with me, dear." The woman holds out her hand, but Janet just stares at her, holding tightly to the cup. "Just leave the cup. Just leave it—don't worry about it."

Janet puts the cup on the table, stares down at the drying vomit on her lap.

"That's right. Don't worry about it. We're going to get you cleaned up."

The woman smiles, wiggles her fingers toward Janet. *Take my hand.*

"Stand up. That's right. It's okay...don't worry."

Janet's ballet shoes slide through vomit that has fallen off the front of her tutu onto the floor.

Again, the woman's fingers wiggle enticingly in space, and Janet's pudgy hand moves toward it, hesitating, until the fingers tentatively connect. Then the woman's hand envelops the small one in a firm, gentle grip.

Holding Janet by the hand, the woman walks toward the exit. Outside the sun shines, white hot and blinding.

The screams of playing children fade into Janet's slow, steady breath as she and the woman whose hand she holds are obliterated by the light.

Chapter 3

Bad News and Vandals

Madeline is in her office at the golf course, preparing the cash deposit for the morning, when she gets the news that the lump on Keira Knightley's side is not cancerous. But before she can process relief at this welcome diagnosis, Dr. O'Sullivan says, in his kind, Irish-accented voice, that unfortunately, however, the tests for the side lump picked up a marker for lymphoma.

Madeline eyes the sleeping, curly brown heap of dog on the round bed at her feet. Keira's feet twitch, and she makes a little, dreamy yip.

"What does that mean?"

"We'll know more once we do a proper blood work-up," Dr. O'Sullivan says. "Don't worry." He pauses. "Yet."

When she ends the call, Madeline reaches out her foot and sinks her bare toes into Keira Knightley's curls. Keira immediately rolls onto her side, inviting a belly rub, and Madeline is gripped by a terrible certainty that Keira is going to die, and it's just all too soon. She lets out an involuntary moan, then claps her hand over her mouth when Keira raises her head to look at her.

"It's okay, baby. Go back to sleep."

Keira flops back and yawns widely.

Madeline turns back to counting the cash, but her mind isn't on it, and by the time she gets to the end of the stack of ones, she's lost count. She sighs, stuffs the cash and deposit slip into the bank bag, zips it and places it squarely in the middle of her immaculate desk blotter. Then she slips on her faux-leather ballet flats and gets up.

Keira rolls into a crouch then slowly gets to her feet, stretching first one back leg, then the other. She shakes off and stares expectantly at Madeline who now holds her lead.

"Shake it, girl," Madeline says. "Let's go."

Raoul is scrubbing the backside of the purple-skinned, polka-dot-skirted T-Rex at *Hole #9—T-Rexy* with a sponge. The recent heavy rain has splattered mud across Rexy's textured fiberglass ass, and it isn't an easy task to get the mud out of those little crevices of faked dino skin. Still, Raoul is patient and doesn't like to rush things. He takes pride in his work, no matter what the task is.

The sky is clear—temperature a little chilly—with ragged, fast-moving clouds, so Raoul hasn't turned on the course floodlights, but unless he finishes soon, he'll be working in the dark. This is why he hates these first few weeks they're open because it costs money to keep the course lighted till seven at night from Thursday through Sunday, and it never pays for itself. Most people aren't interested in golfing when temperatures are still in the low fifties. He's tried to explain this to Kiki over the years, but nevertheless, Schmuck's Mini Golf has always—*always*—opened on April first, whether it's raining, shining or spitting snow just as it has since old Mr. Schmuck built it in 1966.

He rinses the sponge and debates whether to return to the clubhouse for more soap and warm water.

Then he hears voices. Young men, full of testosterone and aggression.

"I'm gonna kick your ass, sucka."

"You wish, bitch."

"Wish bitch...hahahaha."

Madeline will be so pissed off that Kiki let these hooligans in with less than an hour till closing. Sometimes Raoul believes Kiki does these things deliberately to provoke a reaction from Madeline, but he knows if he confronted Kiki about it, she'd just deny it.

Raoul takes a last swipe at Rexy's ass, then leans over and drops the sponge in the bucket. No sense in bothering to go back to the clubhouse now for fresh water. It's already dark enough that he'll need his phone flashlight to walk back. Besides, if these jokers are playing all eighteen holes, the course lights need to be turned on as soon as possible, and he'd prefer to be sitting in his nice, warm office and watching some TV for the next hour while he waits to lock up.

He picks up his bucket and steps up out of the ramped, shallow dell straddling the ten yards from tee to hole that shelters the T-Rex obstacle, sloshing dirty water onto the artificial turf.

"Shit."

Raoul pulls a rag from his back pocket and leans over to sop it up, when a hail of rainbow-colored golf balls burst all around him, one hitting him smartly in the middle of his back.

He straightens up too quickly, wheels around, feeling something give, rather painfully, in his lower back. *Goddammit.*

"Hey!"

"You got him!"

"Faggot!" A gloating laugh. "Faggot in Beaver Town!"

He hears a barrage of choked-off giggles coming from *Hole #4—Beaver Town*. Peering through the gloom, he sees four shadows detach themselves from behind the oversized pair of kissing fiberglass beavers and run off, leapfrogging toward *Hole #7—My Little Pony*.

Raoul hurries back to the front of the park. Kiki is just coming out of the glass-fronted ticket kiosk, carrying a canvas bag over her shoulder.

"What the hell, Kiki?"

Kiki stops. "What?"

"Those kids just threw a damn bucket of balls at me. Little fuckbags." He doesn't mention the slur because even thinking about it stings and enrages.

"What kids?"

"Those *kids*." Raoul waves toward the darkened course, momentarily distracted by the sight of Madeline standing in the spotlights that illuminate the flagpole by the office trailer, as Keira Knightley sniffs and stiffly squats for a pee.

"Raoul, what kids?"

Distant hoots and shouts answer her question.

"Dammit," Raoul and Kiki say at the same time.

Madeline approaches with Keira walking slowly behind her, tail wagging. "Do you hear that? What's going on?"

"It's those goddamn kids," Raoul says to Madeline. "Must've cut through the fence, again."

Madeline frowns, then hands Kiki the lead and says, "Mom, turn on all the lights when I text you." She grabs Raoul's hand. "Let's get the little bastards."

Raoul and Madeline know the course and could walk it blindfolded, but they pick their way carefully in the dark, kicking errant golf balls out of their way as they go.

The kids are now at *Hole #16—The Anteater*. One of them is riding the six-foot-tall fiberglass anteater like a bull.

"Yeehawwww!" they yell and, "Ride that bitch!"

"Kid's gonna bust that he keeps kicking it like that," hisses Raoul.

Madeline hushes him and starts uncoiling the utility hose they use to refill the water trap on *Hole #15—Hello Kitty*. She turns the spigot knob slowly to start the water and the squeak somehow draws the attention of one kid, who turns toward them, peering into the darkness. Madeline goes still, barely breathing. Then, the kid turns back to his friends and shouts, "Slap that bitch hard!"

"Barbarians," breathes Raoul.

Madeline just shakes her head, turns the nozzle to *blast* and sneaks toward the looming anteater, with Raoul right on her heels. She stops short when she sees the same kid turn toward them again—preternaturally attuned to their presence? Or just paranoid. Either way, he's swinging a baseball bat and that's a bad sign.

These kids have been marauding ever since they opened two weeks earlier. No sooner do they repair the fencing than these delinquents cut through in a different section. The damage so far has been minimal, but *this* kid looks like he wants to break something the way he's swinging that bat. They need to move quickly.

Madeline and Raoul creep into the shadow of Hello Kitty. Holding the hose at the ready in one hand, Madeline braces herself against Hello Kitty's blue-bathing-suited bottom, with Raoul so close she can feel his breath on her neck.

"He called me a faggot," Raoul whispers to Madeline. She looks at him over her shoulder, a horrified expression in her eyes. When he nods affirmation, her look back at the boys is murderous.

Baseball Bat Kid swaggers over to the anteater and casually yanks his friend off its back. With a howl, the deposed kid jumps up, fists raised. But Baseball Bat Kid just smiles and hops up onto the anteater's back. He holds the bat between his legs.

"I got a hard on!" he crows.

"Big dick," mutters the kid who got pulled off, rubbing his elbow.

Madeline carefully pulls her phone from her pocket and texts Kiki: *NOW*.

"This bitch loves my big dick!" Baseball Bat Kid yells.

And then the lights come on.

For a moment, a pristine silence. The kids look every which way.

And that's when Madeline aims the hose at the kid riding the anteater and opens the valve on the hose. When the gush of water hits and knocks the baseball bat out of the kid's hands, he's so surprised that he falls backward and slides down the anteater's tail, smashing to the ground on his back.

"Ow!"

And then Madeline turns the hose on all the kids, spraying back and forth, soaking them and, at first, they're so surprised that they just stand there. But then all hell breaks loose, and they're running.

Madeline collects the baseball bat, and she and Raoul walk over to Baseball Bat Kid who's now curled onto his side.

They stand over him. He's moaning, Madeline thinks, rather dramatically.

Raoul says, "You all right? Can you move?"

Baseball Bat Kid says, "Fuck off, faggot" and sits up, wincing a little. Pure hate in his eyes, he jerks his chin at the bat and says, "That's mine."

"Not anymore," Madeline says.

"Fuck you."

Madeline and Raoul look at each other, then Madeline says, "Don't come in here again. Bitch." She swings the bat back and forth and he makes a swipe for it but she's faster than he is, and he grabs air.

Raoul holds out his hand to help the kid up, but he bats the hand away, pulls himself into a crouch, then limps off toward the hole in the fence at *Hole #18—The Wolf(Man)*.

Madeline calls after him. "Bye! Have a nice night!"

She looks at the now-drenched course, then at Raoul. "Good thing it's not going below fifty degrees tonight. We'd be ice-skating out here tomorrow."

Back at the office, a cheery note tells them that Kiki's gone home and taken Keira with her.

"Everything okay, Mads?" Raoul asks while she's putting on her jacket. "You seem...sad."

"I'm fine," she says. She doesn't want to tell anyone about Keira yet.

"We were magnificent tonight," he says.

They grin at each other.

"Night, Raoul."

Chapter 4

Pile It On

Kiki opens the door before Madeline makes it to the top step.

"How'd it go?"

Keira Knightley is right behind Kiki, wagging, which stabs Madeline with fear and a painful punch of loss, even though the dog's not dead, she's standing there, wagging. *She isn't dead.*

"What's wrong?" Kiki asks.

Madeline shakes her head and leans forward to run her hands over Keira's curly head.

"Come in."

Madeline shakes her head again. "I'm tired."

"Well, what happened with the kids?" Kiki steps back, crowding Keira back into the hallway and Madeline is forced to step inside. The storm door clicks shut behind her, but Madeline doesn't follow Kiki when she moves off into the living room.

Her mother calls from the other room, "Close the door. The heat's on."

Madeline closes the door, then shoos Keira ahead of her and goes into the living room. Kiki has a rerun of *Love It or List It,* her favorite home renovation show, on the flatscreen TV that dominates the cramped room, further cluttered by photos in frames on every surface of Madeline and Kiki skiing in the Alps, or Madeline on the beach in Spain, or Madeline with that dyke-y haircut Kiki loathed, holding her college diploma.

Madeline's attention is caught by Hilary Farr, gesturing at the camera and looking desperate, bemoaning the low budget that the homeowners have allowed her. She's not a miracle worker, for heaven's sake! Kiki likes to say that Hilary Farr is her "Astro Twin," whatever that is. Madeline assumes it's like a doppelgänger but less scary. She realizes her mother is watching her.

"What?"

"You look pretty today."

Madeline rolls her eyes.

Kiki hits the mute button, then sits down on the sofa. She pats the space next to her, and Keira jumps up and curls next to her.

"Mom, don't do that. I gotta go."

"Just for a minute, honey. I want to talk to you."

"What about?"

"Can't I just want to talk to you without you suspecting me of something?"

"I *suspect* you want company."

"Pffft," Kiki says. She smiles at Madeline, runs her hand down Keira's curly side. "C'mon, rest your bones."

Madeline sits down on the edge of the sofa, trying to figure out Kiki's game, but her mother isn't giving anything away. "What do you need?"

"I don't *need* anything. What happened with those kids? Did they cut the fence again?"

"We hit them with the hose. They left." Madeline shrugs, then says, "Got a baseball bat off one of them in case they come back."

"What?"

"Yeah. Kid had a baseball bat, but we captured it when he fell off the Anteater after I sprayed his ass."

"Of course you did." Kiki beams at Madeline. "Don't mess with my Mads. She means business!"

"We're going to have to get the fence repaired. I think we need to get creative if this keeps happening. Maybe even hire security."

"They're just kids."

"Destructive foul-mouthed kids who keep wrecking our fence and trespassing on our property." She pauses, then says, "They called Raoul a *faggot*."

Kiki's lips twist in disgust. "Ew. Little shits."

"Right." Madeline starts to get up, but Kiki puts a hand out. "Wait—" She points down at Keira's side, then mouths something at Madeline as she pantomimes a phone call.

"Oh, did I hear from the—yes. They have to do further tests."

Kiki puts her hands over Keira's soft ears. "Well, is it...." she lowers her voice into a whisper, "...cancer?"

Madeline wants to cry. She swallows. "I don't know. Maybe." She stands up. She needs to be alone. Sensing Madeline's distress, Keira pulls herself up and jumps off the couch. She shakes off and trots toward the doorway, looking back over her shoulder to make sure Madeline is coming.

"I'll see you tomorrow, Mom, okay?"

Kiki looks away, shrugs, grumbles about Madeline always rushing off somewhere or other, and how she used to *like* her mother's company, but Madeline doesn't take the bait and determinedly backs away, then turns and follows Keira into the hallway.

"I love you!" Madeline calls when she pulls the door open, but the volume is cranked again, Hilary Farr saying, "Are you going to *love it...*?" and David Visentin's canned response, "Or...are you going to *list it*?"

Madeline feeds Keira a little extra tonight. Why not? Then she microwaves an Amy's Light and Lean black bean and quinoa bowl for herself and pours herself a larger than usual glass of her favorite red wine, a California zinfandel.

Jawari texts her just as she's putting her plate and fork in the dishwasher: *Can I come over?*

Madeline doesn't relish another argument with Jawari after the day she's had, so she texts back: *Really tired. Long day. Tomorrow?* After a long pause of dancing bubbles on her phone screen: *It's important. Won't take long.*

Twenty minutes later, Madeline opens the door. Jawari doesn't smile when she comes in, but she does give Keira ear scratches. Jawari's energy is... cold.

"You going to sit down or what?"

"Do you know what I'm going to say?" Jawari says.

Madeline shakes her head, but maybe she does know.

Jawari paces. "I don't—we can't do this anymore."

"We can't do what? Is this about the commitment conversation?"

"I can't," Jawari says. "I'm not...ready."

Keira Knightley jumps down off the couch and goes to her water bowl, slurping noisily in the silence.

"Okay," Madeline says at last. "I mean...I don't understand, but okay."

But it's most definitely not okay and Madeline wants to break something, so she rearranges the mail lying on her coffee table.

"I've been with someone else."

Madeline looks up. "Since two days ago?"

Jawari's dark eyes water. "I'm sorry, Mads. I care about you but I'm just...."

What? Just what?

Jawari takes a step toward Madeline, her arms open, but Madeline backs away, stifling an urge to vomit. *Do not.* She pivots and goes into the kitchen, pouring herself a glass of water. She swallows it all before turning to face Jawari.

Jawari crouches down next to Keira and slings her arm over Keira's back. Keira leans into her, and Madeline says, "Keira has cancer." Jawari frowns, kisses Keira on the top of her head, then stands up.

"That lump is cancer? Are they sure?"

"Not the lump. It's something else. They don't know yet. We have to do more tests."

Jawari says, "So, once again you're anticipating the worst before you even know the results," and gives Madeline that look, the one she hates.

"Who is she?"

Jawari shakes her head. "I don't want to hurt you. And I don't like cheating."

"Isn't that what you're doing?" Madeline says, "Cheating? I'd call that commitment phobic."

"Maybe you and I went too fast, got into a groove too soon."

"It's been almost a year."

"I warned you I was fickle."

Madeline stares at Jawari who suddenly can't seem to meet her gaze. "You did, but I thought we were tight. In sync. What's going on? For real. Talk to me."

"I'm...."

Jawari looks down at her feet, and the overhead light glints off her glossy black hair. *Her hair.* She's had something done in the forty-eight hours since they spent what was apparently to be their last night together: purple highlights.

"Is it Sasha?" Madeline asks in a hushed voice, because she knows in her bones it's most definitely Sasha. And while she never liked the woman, always got the vibe that Sasha wanted to get between her and Jawari, now she hates her with a white-hot passion.

Suddenly, Jawari moves toward Madeline and pulls her into a tight hug, but her betrayal (*with Sasha*, of all people) stiffens Madeline's spine. She turns her head away, her arms hanging rigidly at her sides.

Jawari sighs and pulls away, gives a final pat to Keira, then goes to the door. Madeline follows her with Keira trailing behind them. At the door, without turning around, Jawari says, "I hope Keira's tests come back negative. Keep me posted."

And she goes out, closing the door softly behind her.

Chapter 5

Leona Now

Leona is in her little office (not much bigger than a cubicle) when her clinical supervisor, Joan, calls and requests a meeting about one of Leona's newer clients, a twelve-year-old girl she's been counseling for almost three months. This girl, Jennifer, has been removed from her mother's house to live with her father and stepmother because the mother is erratic, frequently drunk or on drugs and shows no interest in supervising her daughter. The girl has been engaging in increasingly risky behavior (staying out all night and "playing around" with men). And now, in their latest session (videotaped), Jennifer reveals to Leona that on her last (unsupervised) visit with her mother, they smoked pot together.

Leona knows what's coming when she sees Joan's face (unsmiling) and tense posture. "You didn't report this thing with Jennifer and her mother. Why?"

"I don't want to ruin her life."

"How's that?" Joan's voice drips with sarcasm. "You're required to report this, Leona."

"I was afraid she'd stop coming to counseling. We're making progress."

Joan sighs.

"I was worried about the dad not letting her see her mom. Please don't make the report."

"It's already done," Joan says. "If we didn't report, you risk losing your license. You could face charges. Why is this so personal?"

"The mom is trying." Leona shrugs. "She loves her mother. I don't want to wreck that."

Joan's voice softens. "Let's talk about what this case is bringing up for you."

Leona says, "I'd rather not."

Joan sits back, tilts her head at Leona. "Your history—"

"Is not connected to this," Leona says, but she hears the uncertainty in her own voice. "Maybe you're right."

"If you're triggered by this case, we should reassign."

"Please don't," Leona says. "I'll handle it."

"Your feelings about what happened to your little girl...they're impeding your judgment. I need you to acknowledge that this is getting in your way, so we can help this kid and keep her on track."

The shame and guilt rush at Leona as fresh as it was twenty-five years earlier. She doesn't even realize she's crying until Joan hands her a tissue and says softly, "It's okay. This is good."

She almost cancels her doctor's appointment because she feels so depleted after her crying jag in Joan's office. Despite Leona's repeated assurances that she'll maintain neutrality, Joan goes ahead and reassigns the case. Leona doesn't argue in the end, but she can't help magnifying this failure, even though she understands that it's one of the pitfalls of her profession. *Don't get attached. Maintain appropriate boundaries. Do the job with compassion* and *maintain emotional balance.*

She's holding for Dr. Simmons and is about to hang up when his gravelly voice comes on the line.

"It's important that you keep this appointment," he says. "I need to discuss your chest X-ray results."

He needs to discuss routine chest X-rays required for insurance?

When she gets to his office, the nurse brings her in straight from the reception desk to Dr. Simmons's office, where she's never been until then.

Still, when he gives her the news, she feels faint and lightheaded, her breath noisy in her ears, Dr. Simmons's voice a quiet, soothing drone.

Derek loves Leona's vegan shepherd's pie, so that's what she makes for dinner that night. She waits until he's had a second helping, then brings him a slice of store-bought cherry pie and sits down next to him (instead of across the table). She takes both of his hands in hers.

"I have cancer," she announces. "It's bad, but they think they can treat it, so that's what I'm going to do. I have an appointment with the oncologist next week."

Derek stares at Leona. His hound dog eyes fill with tears.

"It'll be okay," she says, then adds, "We've been through worse together."

That night, lying sleepless next to Derek, Leona is thinking about Janet. She imagines telling her daughter she's dying, imagines Janet holding her, weeping. She sees a gathering around a gravesite. Derek. And Janet. They throw roses into her open grave. Leona stifles a sob, rubs her eyes violently. *Stop.*

When Leona falls asleep, finally, around three in the morning, she dreams that she's with Janet—though she doesn't recognize the person in the dream as *her Janet*—and her daughter is pregnant. She wakes up and thinks, *I could be a grandmother and not even know it.* Everything is pointing her in one, undeniable direction: to try one last time to find Janet.

She vows to start with the only clue she's ever possessed: the woman in the bathroom.

The incident with her client leads to a gentle suggestion from the executive director of the agency that, given her situation, she should resign her position and focus her energy on her health, so she says goodbye to her colleagues at an emotional going away party, then packs her photo of Janet wearing that stupid tutu and a photocopy of the woman in the bathroom's identikit that the police gave her, the bits and pieces of her work life worth saving. The mugs that say things like *Inspire* or *Believe* or *You Got This*, she hands off to her office mates, but she does bring home the beautiful pen set (she never uses) that Derek gave her when she got her certificate in crisis management.

On her way out the door, Joan stops her, wraps her in a hug and says into her ear, "If you need me, call."

With her career boxed up in the trunk, she tells Derek in the car that she doesn't have any regrets, but that isn't exactly true. She would have liked to say a proper goodbye to some of the kids who still keep in touch with her. Jamila and Shah who survived starvation in Mogadishu, only to lose both parents to two different kinds of cancer within two years of their arrival in the US. They had both gotten scholarships to state universities, had excelled despite all the strikes against them, and now Jamila is in medical school while Shah works for a Fortune 500 company as an accountant. Carrie, who had narcolepsy and was shuttled from foster home to foster home after her addict mother was jailed for dealing is now a teacher assistant in the public schools. Daniel, the kid whose dad burned him with cigarettes and who repeatedly threatened to kill himself or his fosters, is in AA and working the steps. Ryan. Siobhan. Veronica. So many damaged children surviving horror and making lives for themselves.

And Janet. Missing now for twenty-five years. *Where was she?*

The private investigator's name is Blair Robinette. She's a tall, capable-looking woman with iron-gray hair pulled into a loose ponytail, wearing an expensive pantsuit, and her smile is friendly and kind as she ushers Leona and Derek into her tidy office.

"I'm nervous," Leona says first thing.

Blair smiles. "No need for that."

After Leona explains—haltingly, with Derek's help—what they want her to do, Blair leans back in her chair and nods solemnly. She doesn't say anything for so long that Derek and Leona exchange a nervous glance.

"Okay," Blair says at last, leaning forward again and placing her hands flat on the desk. She looks from Leona to Derek and back again, then taps the photo of Janet and the identikit drawing. "Let's see if we can give you guys some closure."

Then Leona says, "Janet's alive. I—" she motions between her and Derek, "—we believe that."

"You need to keep your expectations reasonable," Blair says gently. "It's been a long time. But we'll do our best to find out what happened to her."

When Leona and Derek get home from the appointment with Blair Robinette, there's a message on the answering machine from the doctor asking Leona to call them back. Derek holds her hand while she makes the call. When she hangs up, Derek says somewhat impatiently, "Well? What'd they say?"

"My first treatment is on Thursday," Leona says. "They said I should expect to lose my hair."

Derek pulls Leona into his arms and says, "Let's go hat shopping, what do you say?" He kisses her gently on the forehead. "It's going to be okay."

Chapter 6

The Watchers

Kiki has been getting weird hangup phone calls for a couple of weeks now. She had also noticed a dull silver sedan last month, parked down the street, with somebody sitting inside for an hour or two at a time, different times of the day, even at night. The car seemed like a bad omen. Now, the hangup phone calls are unnerving.

She hasn't mentioned any of this to Raoul because she knows what he'll say. That she's being paranoid or dramatic. Sometimes he can be so judgmental, acting the older brother when actually, he's six months younger than she is. He acts like he knows her so well, but Kiki still has a few secrets.

In particular, she's keeping secret that she's had Bernie, their lawyer, draw up the papers transferring her ownership shares of Schmuck's Mini Golf to Madeline and making her the CEO. He doesn't know that she's planning to bow out gracefully at the New Year—at sixty-six, after all, why shouldn't she?— and start living a different kind of life. Less work, more travel. But also, she wants to secure Madeline's future by handing it to her on a silver platter.

Schmuck's has been a moneymaker from Day One, and it still provides a comfortable living and affords them expensive yearly vacations that Kiki insists are the only times she really has a chance to spend quality time with Madeline, even though they work together and live (though in different dwellings) on the same property, within yards of each other.

The living arrangement had come about when, during her college graduation weekend, Madeline had informed Kiki and Raoul that she intended to move into an apartment closer to Philadelphia as soon as she could find one. She announced this during the celebration dinner at Lacroix.

"You'll need to get a roommate," Kiki says.

"Maybe," Madeline says. "Maybe not."

"You'll have a terrible commute," Kiki says. "You hate driving."

"The traffic's going the other way," Madeline counters. "I could also take the train. Raoul can pick me up on his way in."

In a stroke of improvisational genius, and out of desperation to keep

Madeline close, Kiki had proposed renovating the separate brick garage behind the main house into a tiny house where she could live rent free. That had sealed the deal, primarily because it's generally easier to give in to Kiki than fight her. And Madeline clearly enjoys a life of financial security compared to her friends (no student loans, a brand-new car, those yearly junkets to exotic places), thanks to her mother.

Now, when Kiki comes out of the house in her robe to pick up the newspaper—it's barely light out at five thirty—she sees a white sedan, parked on the opposite side of the street, three houses down, in front of the Myers's brick rancher. Seeing it makes her shiver even though the morning air has no bite. She picks up the paper and stands for a moment, staring at the car, willing it to go away. She hugs herself, holding the paper to her chest, then hurries back inside.

Something rank is bubbling up to the surface and she can pretend as much as she wants, but it's there. And it's coming. She can't stop it.

Raoul must have had a few too many cocktails the night before because his head is splitting, and he has terrible cotton mouth. When he comes into the office (late), he goes immediately for his stash of Tylenol Extra Strength caplets and pops two with several small cups of water, one after the other.

Across the room, Kiki eyes Raoul but doesn't say anything until he's poured his coffee.

"I've been thinking about what we were talking about last week," Kiki says. "I'm doing it."

Raoul looks at her over the rim of his mug and takes a cautious sip of the hot coffee. "The retirement thing?"

Kiki nods.

Raoul drinks his coffee, looking at her steadily over the rim of the mug. "What?"

"First of all, you'll hate it." He puts the mug down, gives Kiki a long look, then says, "And these—" air quotes, "'tactics' are not going to get you what you want."

"You don't know what I want."

Raoul laughs. "I think I do."

"What do I want, Raoul," Kiki says with heavy sarcasm.

"You want to trap her. You want her to spend her entire life living in your guest house and running your golf course. Have you ever asked her if she wants to own the business? What about me? Did you think to ask *me* what *I* think about all this?"

Kiki blinks at him.

"Wow." Raoul waves his finger at her. "You're something else."

"I thought you'd be fine with it."

"I'm not."

"I can't talk to you," Kiki sniffs, shuffling papers on her desk.

"Because I'm the only one willing to tell you the truth."

"You're impossible," she says, ending the discussion.

Raoul shrugs, stands up and goes over to the low-slung pleather couch next to Kiki's desk. He lies down and closes his eyes.

Kiki's fingernails tap her cellphone. The mini fridge ticks. There's the faintest sound of early spring bird calls outside. Raoul takes deep, cleansing breaths, letting the Tylenol work its magic on his headache.

"I should buy you out," Raoul says into Kiki's cone of silence. "That's what should happen."

Kiki's fingernails tap-tap away.

"I don't like the idea of those pointy daggers," Raoul says as he and Kiki walk back to the office from *Hole #18—The (Wolf)Man*. They've just met with a security company rep—Steve, blond and aggressively groomed—who is suggesting they replace the old six-foot chain link with a modern eight-foot-high, black-powder-coated, steel fence topped by curved, pointed ends. Raoul doesn't like the look of the glossy, menacing pictures.

"It looks like something you'd put around Fort Knox," he says.

Kiki smiles and nods to three golfers playing through the mountain obstacle on *Hole #12—Wile E. Coyote*, then says, "I didn't know you felt that way."

"And closed-circuit TV or a private security contract are a good idea, but the price tag is ridiculous."

Kiki taps his arm. "About Madeline."

"Madeline? She'll agree with me."

Kiki shoots him a look.

"Shit. We doing this *now*?" Raoul says. He'd rather not because Kiki can be volatile when she's gnawing on resentments, real or imagined.

"Relax," Kiki says. "I'm not mad. And nothing is set in stone."

Raoul laughs. "Well, gee, that's a relief."

They approach the office, and Raoul sees that Madeline's blue VW is in the parking lot. He stops Kiki to say what he needs to say before they go inside.

"I wasn't being serious," he says. "About buying you out."

"Oh," Kiki says. "Okay."

"But I don't understand why you didn't at least ask me."

He offers a hurt smile in Kiki's direction, then turns and goes inside.

When Madeline takes Keira for her noontime walk, Kiki tags along. They talk about the fence and refurbishing the torn Astroturf on *Hole #11—The Little Heifer,* the various options to fill the new vending machine—Madeline favors salty snacks, while Kiki insists chocolate candy is the gold standard of vending machine merchandising. They talk about anything other than what they want to say to each other.

But on their way back, Madeline says, "You may as well know that Jawari and I have broken up." Reading her mother's expression she says, "I knew you'd be happy to hear that."

"I'm not *happy.*"

"You're smiling."

"I'm not."

"You never liked her."

"I didn't *not* like her."

"She's smart. She's beautiful. She's successful."

"Yes, okay. She is…a very nice girl. I just never thought she was right for *you.*"

"Woman," Madeline says. "She's a woman."

"Woman," repeats Kiki.

"She's been cheating on me. With her hair stylist."

"Oh, honey," Kiki says. "I'm sorry. So, she's not so nice, after all."

Madeline shrugs. "It's not black and white, Mom."

Keira stops to sniff a bicycle that's clearly been abandoned, one wheel missing, seat torn, but still locked to the light pole, and Kiki notices the dull silver sedan parked in a metered spot not fifty feet away, near the corner, directly across from Schmuck's parking lot. Is it the same car? She can see from here that the driver's seat is empty. *No watcher. Where's the watcher?*

"Mom? Did you hear what I just said?"

Kiki tears her eyes away from the vehicle.

"Can you come with me when I take Keira to the vet tomorrow morning?"

"Oh—" Kiki blinks at her daughter, looks down at Keira's sweet face gazing up at her. "Yes, of course, I can."

They cross the street, and Kiki can't resist a backward glance at the silver sedan.

"What are you looking at?" Madeline says, turning to see what Kiki's staring at.

"Nothing!" Kiki links arms with Madeline and smiles to hide the sudden lurching terror in her gut.

Chapter 7

Madeline's Dilemma

Keira Knightley is not prone to nerves except at the vet's, where the moment they pull into the parking lot, she begins to quake. By the time they're inside the waiting room, she's a neurotic mess and trying to climb into Madeline's lap. Keira weighs close to forty pounds.

Madeline and Kiki try their best to calm her, but the fifteen-minute wait is excruciating for everybody. Keira's nails scrabble at the slick linoleum, pulling Madeline behind her as they follow Johanna, the vet tech, into Room #3.

Keira's panting signals her internal stress, even though she obediently lies down at Madeline's feet. Kiki stands by the examination table, studying a chart showing nauseatingly realistic pictures of a variety of stool samples. At the top is a cartoon character shaped like a dog poop, wearing sunglasses and what Kiki would characterize as a smirk, with a thought bubble that says, "In search of the perfect poop?"

Kiki turns when Madeline sighs. She studies her daughter, who's resting her cheek against the top of Keira Knightley's head.

"She's going to be okay. Stay positive."

Madeline almost snaps at her mother—she hates pep talks. Then cute, Hobbit-sized Dr. O'Sullivan comes in, and Keira is on her feet, shaking off her anxiety and wagging her tail, still panting, but clearly happy to see her favorite vet. He scrubs at Keira's ears affectionately, then smiles at Madeline and greets Kiki. He's known both of them since Kiki brought Keira— a rescue pup from Louisiana—home for Madeline's twenty-first birthday.

"Let's go over Keira's tests and your options."

That night, Madeline leaves Keira snoring on the couch and crosses the lawn to her mother's back door. She knocks then steps inside. "Mom?" The audio from some renovation show or other blares from the living room. "Mom!"

"In here!" Kiki calls from the living room. Then the volume is turned down to a murmur.

When Madeline comes in, she sits down next to Kiki and takes her hand. Their fingers intertwine. Kiki's hand is dry and warm, comforting. They watch as a woman wielding a sledgehammer almost as big as she is swings it at a wall, punching a good-sized hole and sending out a spray of rotten drywall and dust. Within five minutes, through the miracle of editing and time-lapse, the entire wall is gone. The show goes to a commercial, and Madeline says, "I'm not going to do the treatments, Mom. It's not fair to do that to her."

"I understand." She squeezes Madeline's hand gently.

"I don't want her to suffer through such a traumatic surgery and then all the chemo. It's not right. I just want her to live her best life for as long as she has." Madeline is crying, but she waves away the tissue Kiki tries to hand her. "I'm fine," she says.

"I know you are."

Madeline buries her face in her hands and ugly-cries until Kiki shoves a whole handful of tissues into her hand. Finally, the storm passes, and Madeline is left with wave after wave of numb, fatalistic acceptance. Keira Knightley, her beloved friend, her favorite being in the entire world, her everything is dying, and there is nothing she can do to make that not be true.

They watch the show for a little while in companionable silence. Then Kiki says, "I have some exciting news. I wasn't going to tell you yet, but with you and Jawari and now Keira and—hold on...." She gets up and goes out of the room.

Madeline barely has time to wonder what Kiki's up to before her mother is back, carrying a thick manila envelope. She sits back down on the couch and puts the envelope on Madeline's knees.

Madeline looks at the envelope, noting the printed address of their lawyers in the upper left corner. "What is this?"

"I'm putting you in charge." Kiki taps the envelope with the tip of one neatly manicured nail. "This is the paperwork making you the new CEO of Schmuck's Enterprises. The golf course is yours."

Madeline stares dumbly at her mother. "What are you talking about?"

"I'm retiring," Kiki says. Her eyes are sparkling. She looks so happy.

After the initial shock, Madeline says, "That's—that's amazing, Mom. Congratulations."

"Congratulations to you!" Kiki says and grabs the envelope. She pulls out a ream of bound legal documents, hugs them to her chest, then presents them to Madeline.

Madeline's hands stay folded in her lap. "What are you doing?"

"I'm giving you your future," Kiki says. "Security. You need that, and I can give it to you."

Madeline shakes her head. "I don't want it," she says.

Kiki's smile freezes, and the documents land with a thud on the sofa cushion between them.

"What do you mean, you don't want it. That's ridiculous. It's yours. It's always been yours. We're just making it official."

"I'm not doing it," Madeline says. She stands up. "You can't make me do this if I don't want to."

"I'm not making you do anything," Kiki says with exaggerated patience. She recognizes that Madeline is in one of her stubborn moods, so she has to tread carefully or risk all-out mutiny. "We'll talk about it tomorrow."

"No," Madeline says. "We aren't talking about it. Tomorrow. Or ever. I don't want the business."

Kiki's smile is stretched thin and about to tear.

"I'm leaving."

"Fine."

"I'm leaving *here*." Madeline waves her hand at the room. "I'm moving—away." She has no idea why she's just said this. Her heart thuds away in her chest; she's having trouble thinking.

"That's ridiculous."

"Stop telling me that everything I say is ridiculous. It's insulting."

Kiki draws her chin in and folds her arms.

"I need to go—" Madeline gestures vaguely "—do some things."

She turns and goes out. Kiki doesn't move, even when she hears the door close, even when the next show is *House Hunters International*, a show she despises. She should have known Madeline would behave this way. Her natural impulse was always to push back at Kiki.

She stares at that stack of documents for a long time. She has to rethink this.

Once inside the door, Madeline collapses to the floor. Her heart is pounding in a disconcerting way, and her head feels hot while her hands are icy cold, clenching in her lap. Keira Knightley lifts her head, cocks it at Madeline, then lays it back down and lets out a long grunting sigh, blinking sleepily at her.

Madeline's mind races with scenarios. All of them improbable. All of them terrifying. She will not be bullied by her mother into taking on this responsibility. She's never wanted it and would *never* have asked for it. But where on earth will she go?

She pulls her phone out of her pocket, taps in her security code, opens the phone app. Her finger hovers over Jawari's contact in her Favorites. After a long moment of decision, she clicks "Edit" and deletes Jawari. She's going to have to deal with this alone.

Chapter 8

Leona in New Hope

"It will be her thirty-third birthday next Tuesday," Leona says, staring out the window at the Pennsylvania countryside flashing by the car window, a dizzying blend of shades of green.

She looks over at Derek. "Do you think it's true?"

"What?"

"Is this her?"

Derek shrugs. He's focusing on the traffic rather than on all the possibilities, some of which are worst-case scenarios (which he can easily imagine) or best-case scenarios (which he can't). If Blair Robinette is correct, then not only have they finally found Janet—*miraculously alive and…adult*—they've also found The Woman Who Took Her and has raised Janet as her own. He and Leona are entering uncharted territory on this trip to New Hope, Pennsylvania, and he knows that it could be dangerous (emotionally and physically), but he will always support his wife, just as he has since they were in high school, now going on forty years, without question.

Leona is going through the file Blair has compiled. She pulls out a printed photo downloaded from a social media website of three people standing in front of a small, green-roofed building with a sign above it that reads: 'S CLUBHOUS because it's been cropped. They are each identified by name, written with black Sharpie below their image. The younger woman stands awkwardly, arms crossed, between an older woman and man. She looks out cautiously from under a fringe of bangs, a smile half-formed. The older woman looks into the camera with supreme confidence, and the man smiles goofily.

Leona touches her finger to the photo. "I can't tell if I see Janet in there."

Derek reaches for Leona's hand, squeezes her fingers. "That's what we're here to find out."

"I don't know what to wish for. "

"We don't know anything yet," Derek says, releasing Leona's hand to signal a lane change. "Let's try not to get ahead of ourselves."

A couple of miles later, Leona says, "This all feels so unreal."

"Try not to get yourself worked up. Conserve your strength."

"You're right."

Another ten minutes go by, and Leona says, "If...*if* it's her, do I tell her about her father?"

"Let's take it one step at a time. No need to think about what *might* happen because it *might not* happen."

Leona sighs.

Then Derek notes a road sign for Rest Stop, 2.5 Miles. "I need more coffee. You want something to eat?"

Leona grimaces.

"You have to eat," Derek says. "The doctor says—"

"Stop. I know." She smiles to take the sting out her obvious annoyance. "Make sure you get me something chocolate."

"Dessert first? I can do that."

Derek checks them into the motel—it's cheap but clean—and Leona lies down as soon as they get inside the room because he insists. And she *is* exhausted. She can admit that. They've barely left their house since the chemo started, so seven hours in the car is a lot.

She'd had to get permission from Dr. Sarris, her oncologist, for the trip. That had been only the second time in twenty years she'd told her story to anybody, but she's trusted Dr. Sarris, an open-faced woman in her early forties, since the beginning of all this, her "cancer journey" as the brochures say. And after she explains why she has to travel, Dr. Sarris not only doesn't ask too many questions, but she asks their permission to touch base with a colleague in Philadelphia about Leona's diagnosis, in case anything happens while they're gone and need medical attention in a hurry.

Non-small cell lung cancer. That morning in Dr. Sarris's well-appointed office, six months earlier, the words hit like a hail of rocks.

Leona feels herself flinch, Derek's fingers tightening around her own.

"There are lots of options for treatment," Dr. Sarris says briskly. "There's no need to even begin to speculate on 'how long' you have. We have many effective weapons in our arsenal, and depending on how you respond to the treatment regimen, years of life ahead of you."

Most of what she says at that initial consult washes over both Leona and Derek as if she's speaking a different language, but they both hear the positivity in her tone, and later that day, lying together in bed, they promise each other they are only going to focus on the immediate future and not worry about the *future* future.

After she quits her job, Leona has a lot more time on her hands. Time for thinking. Regrets. Reliving painful memories that still tear at her, so many years later, in waking dreams, in glimpses of familiar-seeming faces that always turn out to be strangers.

One day, while she's in the middle of a chemo transfusion, while she's listening, eyes closed, to her favorite Chillwave Pandora station, while she focuses on picturing a flag-waving welcome by her open veins of the cancer-killing poison, she's suddenly back in that bathroom with the smell of industrial cleaner and Janet's vomited pizza in her nostrils, the screaming laughter of children in her head, and the woman's clear blue eyes rimmed by stubby lashes, watching her in the mirror, judging her, deciding she's unworthy.

The next morning, over coffee, she had told Derek she wanted to hire a private investigator to find Janet. Now, five weeks and $10,000 later, Blair Robinette has turned in her startling report that, in fact, there is a strong possibility that the woman in the bathroom has been located and that she has a daughter the exact age that Janet would be.

"It's Janet," Leona says, staring hard at Blair Robinette. "I know it." She turns to Derek, "We need to go find her."

"I don't think that's a good idea," Blair says, throwing a quick worried glance at Derek, who avoids making eye contact.

"This is something you should let the local authorities handle," Blair says sternly. "Get yourselves a lawyer. Play this out officially, a court-ordered DNA test—"

"I'll know if it's her," Leona says. "I don't need any DNA test."

"If this is the woman, then she committed a serious crime, and you should have some support." Another appealing look from Blair to Derek, but he resolutely keeps his gaze on his wife.

"Yes," Leona says. "And I don't give a shit about that bitch right now. We're going to Pennsylvania to find Janet."

Leona often thinks about her cancer as a flame in her lungs that the doctors are trying to put out. She hadn't ever really thought about breathing—about each individual breath—until after her diagnosis. Now, it's all she thinks about, especially when she's lying down—on her side per doctor's orders—and especially when she's stressed. Those people who say, *Just breathe* or *Focus on the breath* as if it's so easy have clearly never had lung cancer.

So here they are. In New Hope. Leona can't help but see a karmic link between the name of the town where Janet now lives—*she lives*—and where, perhaps, at last, they will be reunited. A prodigal mother returned to claim her lost child.

Chapter 9

Strange Behavior

Madeline decides to take her morning walk with Keira at New Hope cemetery, where she knows few people will be this early in the day, barely light outside. She's loading Keira into the car—half lifting, half pushing—when her phone rings. She tosses Keira's lead in after her, closes the door and slides to answer.

"Hi, Mom."

Kiki says, "Good morning. Going for a walk?"

Madeline swings around. Kiki is inside, in her kitchen bay window, waving.

"Yep."

"Well, be careful."

"Mom."

"You never know."

Madeline disconnects, shoves her phone in her pocket, and peels out of the driveway in reverse.

When she and Keira Knightley arrive at the cemetery, she sees Raoul's Audi sedan already parked just inside the gate. She pulls in front of the other car and, holding the support handle on her harness, helps Keira make a soft landing from the back seat. She snaps Keira's leash onto the D-ring on her halter, and they walk into and under the early spring canopy, sunrise just beginning to sparkle the dew on the grass, past a row of broken, ancient tombstones toward the first right turn: Eastern Lane.

Raoul is sitting on the low steps of their favorite mausoleum—the name ANDREWS carved into the stone over the bricked-in, arched doorway—smoking the single daily cigarette (American Spirits, blue hard pack) that he allows himself now that he's "quit."

The moment Keira sees Raoul, her tail plays double-time, and she whimpers and strains at the leash. Madeline unhooks her, and Keira wiggles the last ten yards to greet Raoul with little, excited jumps on her front feet (because of her arthritic back) and attempted licks of his hand (which she knows isn't allowed).

Raoul scrubs Keira's ears, then her sides, stands up, butts his cigarette and pockets the filter in his plaid blazer with the leather elbow patches.

"Good morning, Professor," Madeline says.

"This old thing?" he laughs. "This is for the married guys who like their boyfriends to pass."

This is an old joke with standard beats they replay each spring when he pulls this particular jacket "out of the closet" as a between-seasons layer.

"I wasn't expecting you today for some reason," Madeline says with a sly, sidelong look.

"Yeah...my date? He wasn't all that. I went home early and got into bed with me, myself and I. I was fabulous."

They walk in companionable silence with the peacefully sleeping dead, listening to the excited awakening birds while the sun comes all the way up. Then the light is too dazzling in their eyes, so they take a left on Viburnum Lane to have its warmth on their backs. Keira is sometimes ahead, sometimes behind, sometimes shuffling parallel through dead leaves and new shoots.

Raoul says, "Your mom called me last night. She says you said you're leaving."

Madeline lets out an angry puff of breath. "She told you?"

"You know how she is," Raoul says.

"Yeah," Madeline says. "Impossible."

They take another left—onto Western View Lane—heading back toward the cars. Madeline whistles for Keira and sees she's squatting for her morning constitutional. Madeline walks over, pulling a poop bag from the back pocket of her sweatpants, and retrieves the poop (*normal, thank goodness!*), then reattaches Keira's leash.

"Let's go, girlie."

They walk, and Raoul says, "You're not really leaving. Are you?"

"Yes," Madeline says, then adds, "Someday."

"If you go, I'm going. Wouldn't be the same without you."

"She has the worst timing," Madeline says.

"You mean, doing this when you've just broken up with your lover?"

"Please don't use that word," Madeline says. She hates that word. *Lover.* What a bullshit concept. "Besides, I didn't break up with Jawari. She *cheated* on me."

"Monogamy is hard, darling. Ask every straight guy I've ever fucked."

"You know what sucks?"

Raoul links his arm through Madeline's and pulls her to his side with a leering look. "Tell me what sucks."

"I'm serious."

"Okay. Seriously, what sucks?"

"Having expectations. Living up to expectations. All of it just…sucks."

Raoul squeezes her arm. "Doesn't it, just?"

"And she knows I'm not going anywhere. Not while…" she cocks her head toward Keira trotting at her side, "…you know."

Before they part, Raoul says, "Your mother takes it for granted that everybody's just going to do what she wants."

Madeline is startled by his grim tone, even more startled when he doesn't say goodbye.

Kiki sits in her car in her driveway, eyeing the silver-blue Toyota Camry parked across the street in her rearview mirror. Two people in the car, their faces turned toward her. She's pretending to let the car warm up, but it's really that she's trying to wait them out, hoping they'll drive off.

When Madeline's car pulls into the driveway next to her, Kiki is relieved to be interrupted in the standoff. She turns her car off and gets out, going around to Madeline's driver's side window.

"Hey."

Kiki peers into the opened window past Madeline, at Keira. "How's she doing?"

"Fine."

Kiki steps back, puts her palms on the door frame. "Are you still mad?"

"I'm not mad."

Kiki rolls her eyes. "Okay, well…I'm over it, okay? I told Bernie I'm not going forward with it." She sighs dramatically. "Obviously."

It's not at all obvious to Madeline, but she says, "Okay, good." Then, "You headed to work? This early?"

"I have some stuff to do, and I told Raoul I'd open. He had a date last night." Kiki curls her lip a little.

"Jealous?"

"He wishes," Kiki sniffs, pushing herself away from the car. She sidesteps to the open back window and ruffles Keira's topknot. "Who's my baby?" she murmurs, then casually, oh-so-casually, glances toward the street, just as the parked car is now slowly pulling away. She can't help staring. It's a man at the wheel and a woman in the passenger's seat who cranes forward, then backward, to keep her and Madeline in her sights as they drive off. Kiki shivers.

Madeline has gotten out of the car and is standing behind her mother.

"Who's that?"

Kiki jitters, takes a shaky breath. "What?"

"That car."

Kiki's already walking off. She's got her head tucked down and her arms held stiffly at her sides. Madeline realizes that her mother is afraid of something.

"Mom? What's going on?"

Without answering, Kiki opens the door to her car, slides behind the wheel, and slams the door. Then the car's in reverse and *gone,* and by the time Madeline gets Keira out of the car, the bright sun has been replaced by banks of scudding, dark clouds. Whose bright idea was it to ever open before May first? This was turning into a real shit of a day.

Chapter 10

Strangers When We Meet

It seems inevitable that, when she pulls into the parking lot at the course, the silver-blue Camry is already there, its motor idling, sending plumes of heavy metal pollution into the atmosphere, another reason (*excuse*) to cling to the chip on her shoulder against whoever was stalking her. *Polluters.*

As Kiki looks out the driver's side window, the woman in the passenger's seat gets out. She's dressed in a plain gray skirt and white sweater, and her silver hair is pulled into a severe bun secured at the nape of her neck. She leans over and speaks to the driver, then closes the door.

Kiki gets out of her car, faces the woman.

"What are you doing here?"

The woman smiles slightly. "Good to see you, Dawn."

Kiki looks over her shoulder. There's no one except the two of them. She says, "Don't call me that. That's not my name."

"You'll always be Dawn to me."

As if butter wouldn't melt… "What do you want?"

The woman spreads her hands out, palms up, she frowns. "Our father has died," she says.

Kiki hears her own breathing, too fast, too harsh and too loud. She feels dizzy. She leans back against her car, the cold metal penetrating her spring-weight fleece jacket.

"I thought you should know." The woman takes a step toward Kiki, stops. "You have a husband and daughter, I see. My niece. Aside from Jakob's girl, she's the only one in the family."

"She isn't—" Kiki clears her throat. Her voice is a croak. "He's not—" She stops, tries again. "Dead? Really?"

"Cancer," the woman says, looking at Kiki as if she's not quite right in her mind. Which, perhaps, is an accurate assessment of her at the moment. "It was quick," she says. "Merciful."

Merciful. "How did you find me?"

The woman performs that little lift at the corner of her lips again, then says, "Facebook."

Kiki stares at her eldest sister, Rebekah, the one who left first, whom she hasn't seen in more than fifteen years anyway, both of them having left for their own reasons, and the last occasion of their meeting so memorably appalling that only something so monumental as their father, Ezra, dying at the ripe old age of ninety-seven would have brought her here. All Kiki can manage to say is, "You're on Facebook?"

Rebekah Miller chuckles with genuine amusement. "I'm as *English* as you seem to be."

Kiki's heart rate is slowly returning to normal until she sees Madeline's VW pulling up to the stoplight at the corner.

"You have to go," she says. "This isn't a good time."

Rebekah stares at her, then shrugs. She turns and steps over to open the door of the car, still idling, still spewing pollution.

"Thank you for letting me know," Kiki says, but she's not sure Rebekah has heard her because she's already gotten into the car and closed the door. Her sister doesn't turn to look at Kiki this time when the car reverses and waits to pull onto the roadway.

Meanwhile, Madeline's car swings past the Camry, and Kiki sees Madeline give a little wave to the car.

Then they're gone.

Madeline parks and gets out of her car. "Who is that?"

Kiki's cheeks are flushed, smeared red blotches radiating toward her neck.

"Are you all right?"

"Hot flash," Kiki says.

Madeline looks surprised. "Okaaayy...so who were those people in the car?"

"Salespeople."

Madeline looks at her watch. "At eight thirty in the morning? That's weird."

Kiki says, "Yep. They won't be back."

The weather stays on the edge of rain, and only two sets of golfers show up to play a short time after they open at eleven: regulars Barry and Darrell, two elderly gentlemen who golf every Wednesday during the season, rain or shine, as long as the course is open. The other is a lively, team-building group (*ten tickets!*) wearing identical crewneck T-shirts that say, Add Spark to Your Life with Sparks Printing and Duplication over a fireworks graphic.

It's cold and damp in the ticket kiosk, and Kiki perches on the high stool with the electric heater glowing red at her feet, hands tucked into her sweater sleeves. She alternates between thinking about her dead father and the last time she'd seen Rebekah, and both make her cringe, a still-raw sense of shame squeezing her gut. *It never goes away. It just hides inside you.*

"Two adults," the man says.

Kiki forces a wide smile, but the couple standing at the ticket window don't smile back. In fact, they seem almost unfriendly. The woman stares at her with open hostility. *Rude.*

"Welcome to Schmuck's!" Kiki says briskly. "That's twenty-two dollars for eighteen holes—will that be cash or credit?"

The man silently fishes money from his pants pocket, counts out the bills and pushes a twenty and two ones across the polished wood of the ticket booth counter top.

"You folks from around here?" Kiki slides the bills into the cash drawer, hits Print Receipt.

The man looks at the woman. They both shake their heads.

"Where you visiting from?"

A pause; then the woman says quietly, "Niagara Falls."

"Oh, I love Niagara Falls," Kiki says, and pushes two ticket stubs and a receipt toward the man. "Been there quite a few times."

The woman turns abruptly—(*again!*) rudely ignoring Kiki's friendly overtures—and walks off toward the chain link turnstile leading to the first hole. The man follows her quickly. Kiki watches as they push through, choose clubs (purple for him, light green for her) and pick matching balls from the racks just inside the fence.

She watches as they huddle for a moment. *Odd.* When they both look back at her, Kiki waves and smiles reassuringly, and then they turn and walk over to tee up for *Hole #1—Hog Heaven.* He lets the woman play first, but she's terrible, and her ball goes wild into the molded fiberglass mud trap.

She's not sure why. but these two give her a funny feeling. and between that and having to deal with Rebekah—*and the fact that he's dead, finally, really, forever dead!*—she doesn't immediately answer when Madeline calls and asks if she wants to go to lunch and talk things out.

"Mom, *what* is going on today? You're acting weird."

"Yeah, I know. I'm just not—hungry."

Silence, then Madeline says, "I'm sorry I'm such a disappointment."

"You are not a *disappointment.* You're an incredibly smart, capable woman. You can do anything you want."

"But I can't be what *you* want."

Kiki grips the phone. "I just want you to be *happy*."

"I'm *happy*. I think."

They both laugh at that.

"Did you take some kind of pill or something?"

Kiki can feel tears building. "I have to go," she says.

"Mom? You okay?"

"Life is too short to be forced into doing something you don't want to do," Kiki says in a rush and disconnects.

Her tears are not about *him—he's dead, gone forever!*—but seeing Rebekah has scraped at the hardened scar tissue covering those old wounds, and the pain feels as fresh and nauseating now as it did when the wounds were inflicted.

What goes around comes around.

Let her go.

Madeline stares at the phone in her hand. What the fuck is going on with her mother? She'd expected to have to bring out her laundry list of reasons why she wasn't ready/didn't want the responsibility/absolutely had no intention of being "in charge" of Schmuck's Mini Golf. This was Kiki's dream. But it wasn't—has never been—hers, and now, with Keira at death's door (even if that door winds up staying closed for weeks or, hopefully, even a few months), Madeline feels the ground shifting beneath her tidy, complacent life.

No, she doesn't have a plan. No job prospects. No place to go to, yet. But if her mother is truly giving up this idea of retirement and Madeline taking over the business without a fight, then maybe, this time, she should finally break away, live her own life, find out who she is on her own. The possibilities (and the fear) make her breathless and jumpy with adrenaline.

She whistles, low, and Keira blinks at her sleepily from her warm bed.

Outside, the sky is still relentlessly gray, so Madeline herds Keira toward the grassy area on the back side of the office (which is basically a parked trailer painted with SCHMUCK'S ENTERPRISES in candy-colored letters across its broad side) with a flagpole planted outside in a skirt of concrete. Despite the shitty weather, with her mother being so reasonable and Keira seeming *just fine, not sick at all*, this is now turning out to be a pretty good day, a day with *potential* even.

"Hello."

A woman's voice behind her. Madeline turns. The woman is bird-like with prominent, knobby collarbones and Lucille-Ball-red, shoulder-length, bobbed hair (an obvious wig). She's wearing a navy-blue trench coat that's at least a size too big and navy-blue tights on her skinny legs, sensible joggers on her feet. The man wears beige from top to bottom: polo shirt, slacks, short golfing jacket. They both stand there, leaning on their clubs.

Keira looks up, wags and keeps sniffing around, trying to make a decision, and Madeline says politely, "Can I help you? This is the office." She smiles and points helpfully in the direction of the clubhouse. "There's refreshments in the clubhouse next to the ninth hole if that's what you're looking for."

"Are you the owner?"

Madeline smiles. "Nope. I just work here."

The woman frowns, glances at the man. "Aren't you the daughter?"

"Oh, well, yes. I'm the daughter, I guess." Madeline laughs because she's suddenly uncomfortable with the way the woman is staring at her.

The man takes a step toward Madeline, smiles nervously. "We enjoyed— the golf," he says.

Having done her business, Keira ambles toward the strangers.

"Who's this?" the woman says in that voice people use for cute animals.

"Keira, come here!" Madeline says, and when Keira ignores her and goes right over to the woman, she adds, "Sorry!"

The woman waves her off. "She's friendly, aren't you?" She squats to pet Keira while the man stands protectively over her. His cheeks are bright red. *Embarrassed for himself or his wife?*

The woman looks up at Madeline. "Keira's a pretty name. What's your name?"

"I'm Madeline."

The woman's eyes are shiny. She licks her lips. "Like the little girl in the book."

Madeline stomach does a weird flippy thing, looking into the intense, watering eyes of this woman. For a moment, nobody says anything. Then, the man leans down and gently takes the woman's elbow to bring her to her feet. He slips his arm around her waist. "We should go, babe," he says. She nods but keeps her gaze steady on Madeline. Keira stands between them and Madeline, looking back and forth, wagging eagerly.

"Thanks," the man says, drawing the woman away.

"Nice to meet you," the woman says over her shoulder.

"Sure," Madeline says, "you too."

Chapter 11

Leona, 1992

Leona stays in the restroom for a few more minutes, hoping an employee has already taken charge and cleaned Janet off, but just in case she grabs a hefty handful of paper towels.

She winds her way through the restaurant and finds only the cup of vomit left on the table. She's grossed out but not worried because they must have taken Janet somewhere to clean her up.

Leona leaves the mess and goes back to the counter area, waiting in line for her turn.

"My kid threw up," she says to the skinny kid in response to his, "What can I get you?"

The skinny kid looks at her blankly.

"Where is she?" Leona asks, enunciating each word.

"Where's who?"

"My kid."

"I don't—" He stops, cocks his head. "Do you want to order some food, ma'am?"

"Look," Leona says with exaggerated patience, "my daughter threw up her lunch, and I went into the bathroom to get paper towels..." she holds up the wad of towels "...but she's not over there." She gestures toward the table where they were sitting.

"I'll get the manager." He lopes off through a door into the kitchen.

Leona waits. She feels eyes on her, but she ignores that. She's used to being judged.

The kid comes back with a harried-looking redhead.

"How can I help you, ma'am?" she asks.

"Where's my kid?" Leona says.

"Ma'am?"

Leona stares at the woman, the kid. She wraps her arms around herself, suddenly cold. Then she drops the paper towels, turns and runs through the crowded restaurant yelling Janet's name.

She bursts out the door, almost knocking down some granny with kids trailing her like ducklings. She stops. Screams Janet's name. People are staring. She tears through the parking lot to the car. It's empty. She turns, screams Janet's name again, then tears back toward the restaurant.

She pushes her way through the gathered patrons, feeling like her feet are shod in cement, everything slowed way down.

The manager is coming through the crowd toward her. Leona collapses with a wail into her arms. People close in, their faces ballooning around her. Above the whooshing in her ears, she hears the manager say, "The police are on their way."

They bring her home in a cruiser and tell her they'll return her car in the morning in the event they don't find any "evidence" in it.

She knows what they think of her. It's in every judgmental glance and accusatory question about why she left Janet alone at the table. She keeps insisting it's not her fault—Janet knows better than to wander off or take candy from a stranger, for god's sake. She keeps telling them they're wasting time, that whoever took Janet is getting away.

Farther and farther away.

The apartment is cold, but when she turns off the air conditioning, it's too quiet. She doesn't like the thoughts that keep crowding her mind, so she pours herself a mind-numbing quantity of Wild Turkey and lies down on top of her bed with her shoes on. Just in case.

Later, she gets up and walks carefully into Janet's room. She sits on the bed, pets the top cover, then lies down, letting her feet hang over the bottom. It smells like Janet. She wants to cry, but the tears don't come. She knows this isn't normal—she should be crying, rending her clothes, inconsolable—but at least she's alone, so nobody's there to stare and point out that her response is inappropriate.

Like that woman in the bathroom.

Suddenly, Leona sits up. That woman in the bathroom had stared at her like she was a cockroach. She closes her eyes, trying to bring back a mental picture of the woman. Gray slacks. A white sweater...or maybe it was a white shirt. She was very plain. No jewelry, no makeup. She'd noticed that.

She opens her eyes again. Somehow this brief encounter with the woman in the bathroom seems significant, and she hasn't told the cops about it.

Because she's had too much Wild Turkey by now, and because she knows only one person she can trust not to accuse her of being a bad mother by letting her kid get taken from a Chuck E. Cheese, she calls Derek. Thank god he sounds sober when he picks up.

"I need you to take me down to the police department."

"Okay," Derek says. "Why?"

"Janet's...gone."

"What?"

"I don't have time to explain everything right now. Can you just come? Please?"

When Derek pulls up out front, Leona's waiting outside. It's a cool evening but not cold enough to warrant Leona wearing a winter parka with fake fur trim on the hood and wrists.

"Thanks for coming," Leona says, her teeth chattering.

"What the hell happened?" Derek asks.

Then Leona bursts into sobs.

"I was...irritated with her," Leona says flatly. "She threw up and I..." Her voice trails off, and Derek takes her hand.

They've been sitting there for the past hour and a half, going over and over it, and still nothing makes sense. And Janet is still gone. Derek feels helpless, but he can't help also feeling glad that, of all people Leona could have called, it was him she chose.

"We're going to get her back," he says.

Leona shakes her head. "I shouldn't have been so...mean. I don't know why I do that."

Derek squeezes Leona's fingers and says nothing. He's seen the two of them, and he knows how Janet can, as Leona puts it, dance on her mother's last nerve just by existing. In that sense, he feels a certain kinship with the little girl, having been the target of Leona's wrath more than once. And when he has witnessed Leona harshness and impatience with Janet, he has taken the little girl aside to reassure her that Leona's tendency to act out is born of frustration, and to explain that *no, she doesn't hate you.*

Leona was like a caged animal that lashed out because she felt *trapped.* Derek has had plenty of time to consider what motivates Leona's rage, so easily sparked, has spent many hours thinking about it, in fact. Leona had been born with ambition, brains and grit but no opportunity to develop her native talents, and wasn't that sad? He doubts Janet understands these excuses he makes, on Leona's behalf, for her indifferent mothering, for her rages and tirades. Sometimes he noticed the little girl had this tendency to "zone out" or disconnect, which unfortunately only exacerbated the tension between them.

This is a mess, Derek thinks. *This whole thing is a terrible mess.*

Leona says, "They're going to blame me."

"Who?" Derek asks. "Nobody would do that. It was the middle of the day. At a restaurant for kids." The minute he says it, he wishes he could take it back. Of course, a restaurant *for kids* might attract the worst kind of predator.

Leona wants to throw something, break something, hurt something. And no matter what goddamn Derek wants to believe, they're going to blame her for losing her kid. Goddamn Derek. Goddamn Janet. Goddammit. This is her fault. She knows it.

At the station, a sleepy desk sergeant escorts them up the stairs to the Criminal Investigation Division where a sharply dressed Detective Stone meets Leona and Derek (who insisted on coming inside with her). He takes in Leona's coat, runny nose and red-rimmed eyes, and takes them into a small conference room.

"We're doing everything we can, Ms. Russo," Stone says once they're all seated around the table. He looks at Derek. "And you are...?"

"I'm here for moral support," Derek says.

"Your name, sir?" Stone says, pen poised over his little black notebook.

After Derek sullenly provides his name, Stone turns again to Leona.

"Why are you here?"

"I thought of something."

Stone waits.

"There was a woman. In the bathroom. She..." Leona stops. What can she say about that woman to convince this cop it's worth his time?

"She...what?" prompts Stone.

"She—we talked for a couple minutes. We had a conversation," Leona finishes lamely.

"Uh-huh."

"Actually, she didn't say much. Or—anything, really. It was her eyes."

"Her eyes."

"She was looking at me like this."

Leona leans forward, lowers her chin, and looks critically at Stone.

"Do you think this woman might have taken your daughter?" Stone asks.

Leona sits back, lets her breath out in a puff, shrugs. "It was weird. The way she looked at me."

Derek says, "Maybe she should look at mugshots, see if this lady's in there."

Stone's lips tighten into a disapproving line. "A woman is in the bathroom at the same time as you. She doesn't say anything to you. I don't see where this goes."

"It means something," Leona says quietly. "I know it."

When Derek drops her back at home, Leona doesn't immediately get out of the car.

Not looking at him, she asks if he wants to come in, but Derek makes some poor excuse about having to get up early (which Leona knows is a lie—she's broken his heart too many times). Then he says, "They'll find her. Don't give up hope."

They don't say goodbye when she gets out of the car. She watches him drive away, then turns and goes inside.

Leona sleeps in Janet's bed. More accurately, she lies awake in Janet's bed. In the morning, she feels like shit, not just because of all the Wild Turkey, but also because she knows she will soon have to tell everybody that Janet is gone.

After three days and multiple, hours-long interviews with the police, they apparently decide that Leona is not a suspect.

But it's still her fault. And Janet is still gone.

Has it really been three weeks? Lying in bed, staring at the outline of light around the window shade, Leona tries to think what day it is. She rolls over away from the light and squeezes her eyes shut, but she can't sleep when it's light outside. Her kitchen phone rings. And rings.

That will undoubtedly be Derek. Or work. Mr. DiStefano had called her on Friday to awkwardly inquire when she might be returning to work. She hadn't picked up, but he'd left a message. She hears her answering machine click on, her outgoing message comes on and she hears Janet's voice, tentative but on script: *You have reached Leona and Janet. Leave us a message!*

Now Derek's voice: *It's me. Give me a call. I'm off today. Thought we could go for a ride.* There's a brief pause, then: *Call me, okay? Please?* and the machine clicks off. Silence, blessed silence.

It's Monday.

Just being able to know what day it is gets her to open her eyes. She's thirsty, but drinking the rest of the Wild Turkey sitting right there on the bedside table isn't a good idea, so she drags herself out of bed and goes into the kitchen. But, of course, there's no coffee, just a box of stale Lipton tea in the cupboard. There's about an inch of orange juice in the fridge, but she hates orange juice, only buys it for Janet because of the vitamin C, so she opts for tap water.

She thinks about having to go to the grocery store, and the thought is terrifying. Since the kidnapping, there are occasions when people recognize her. The looks she gets make her paranoid. *They* think she's a bad mother too. It's obvious they don't understand that it wasn't *her* fault.

It was her fault though.

Derek is the only one who doesn't see her as some kind of monster. She picks up the phone.

He sounds breathless and relieved when he answers. "Want some company?"

Does she really? Won't it give him the wrong idea? Still, even though he's one of the least exciting people she knows, he's also the most dependable, and there are times when it just feels good to be loved.

"How about that drive?" she says.

She doesn't talk much on the ride to the falls, but Derek doesn't seem to need her to (a relief) and just puts in her favorite CD (*Let's Get Rocked* by Def Leppard). They wait in a long line for tickets for the Hurricane Deck, don their yellow ponchos, allowing themselves to be carried along by the crowd, and at one point, Derek takes her hand, and she doesn't pull away.

The water rushes in front, above, behind, the noise of the cascade and the excited children washing over them. At one point on the walkway, Leona grips the handrail, lets the water pummel her face and body, held steady by Derek's hand at her waist.

Back in the car, they towel off (he's thought of *everything*) and when Derek goes in for the kiss, she lets that happen too.

After that, they're officially an item, but Leona doesn't tell Derek that when she got back from their Niagara Falls adventure, she'd been let go—by answering machine—from her job as the counter person at DiStefano's Dry Cleaning, Mr. DiStefano explaining that such a public-facing job might not be a good idea for her *at this point in time*. She'd told the answering machine to go fuck itself. It was clear that she'd have to do something soon or be evicted.

Meanwhile, the two FBI agents who had *interrogated* her in the aftermath of the kidnapping decide to pack up their fancy black briefcases and go back to Buffalo. The case was still open, but police had no leads. Janet had vanished.

There are days following this latest non-development when, at Derek's urging, Leona makes calls to various media outlets in the area and to her state and federal legislators. Everyone is sympathetic. They feel her pain (*no, they don't*) and want to help (*they don't*), but it's a police matter, and she should let them handle it. One of the national network affiliates sends a reporter to speak to her, but nothing comes of the story other than a brief mention at the end of a broadcast where they put up Janet's school picture from last year (the only one she could find) and offer the FBI Tip Line phone number for anyone who has any information.

Her life at a standstill, Leona moves out of the two-bedroom apartment she can no longer afford into Derek's smaller one-bedroom across town. He doesn't ask—or expect—her to pay rent or contribute anything toward bills, but Leona has *some* pride, so she starts looking for a new job, even managing to get a couple of interviews, but nothing seems to stick, and most days she now spends in front of the TV, waiting for Derek to get home.

Derek gets home late that day, and the apartment windows are dark which doesn't, immediately, alarm him. But when he comes in the apartment and hears water running in the bathroom, his synapses fire alarm, and he rushes to the door (left ajar) and pushes it open.

"Hi," Leona says. She's lying in the tub with only her face above water. Her hair fans out around her, Medusa-like.

Derek's heart is hammering, and he doesn't trust himself to speak. He walks over, lowers the toilet seat and sits down.

"What's going on?" Derek says.

Leona sits up and turns off the water. She hugs her knees to her chest.

Derek wants to run his finger down her spine, touch every vertebra.

"I'm going to check myself into the hospital," Leona says. "Will you drive me?"

Chapter 12

Kiki, 1992

She knows there isn't much time, so when they get to her car, she helps the little girl into the back seat and straps her in without bothering to clean her off.

When she gets behind the wheel, she opens all the windows and takes gulps of fresh air to avoid feeling nauseated by the smell, then backs quickly out of the spot. She has to wait for a woman herding four toddlers on leashes before she can pull onto the access road and make her getaway.

"Where are we going?"

The woman looks in the rearview mirror. "Home."

Janet stares at her, and the woman drags her attention back to the road. "You're going to be very happy there," she says. "You'll have your very own dinosaur."

Janet looks away, out the window. Her lower lip trembles.

"Don't you like dinosaurs?"

Janet shrugs.

"I'm Kiki," the woman says to Janet's reflection in the rearview.

Janet turns her head to look at her. "Is my mom going to be there?"

"Where?"

"At...at home."

"Do you want her to be there?" Kiki asks.

Janet nods, bites her lip.

"Okay, Janet. We'll see. But until then, I want you to know you're safe and we're going home. I think you'll like it."

"Because of the dinosaur?"

"Oh, there's lots more to like. You'll see."

"Okay." Janet turns and stares out the window again.

Kiki pulls into the next rest stop and, taking Janet by the hand, marches her into a single-stall bathroom and cleans her off as best she can. She dries the wet spots on the ratty tutu by putting Janet right under the hand dryer. Then they go into the gift shop and Kiki tells Janet to pick out a new outfit.

Janet has never been consulted about her clothes. But when Kiki presses her, she points at a Harry and the Hendersons sweatshirt, and even though it's miles too big for Janet, Kiki slings it over her arm and says, "It'll make a very cute dress! Good job."

Kiki also buys a three-pack of anklet socks in black, white and pink, a small plastic hairbrush, and a pair of hair scissors. At the register, she tells Janet to pick out a hair clip from the display on the counter. Janet points at a crystal-encrusted hair comb that would be highly unlikely to stay put in her fine light brown hair, but Kiki adds it to the pile. She also selects a two-pack of small butterfly clips in pale mauve.

After their purchases, Kiki takes Janet back to the single-stall bathroom and changes her out of her puked-on dress into the sweatshirt, which reaches below Janet's knees. She helps Janet roll up the sleeves, then wets the little girl's hair with her hands and trims it with the new scissors to chin length with Dutch Boy bangs, the same haircut as Kiki. She smiles at herself over Janet's head in the mirror.

"I think you look very nice," Kiki says, turning Janet toward the mirror, "What do you think?"

Janet looks at herself and a small smile plays at the corner of her mouth. Kiki puts the heavy crystal hair comb in Janet's hair, anchoring it with the two butterfly barrettes. "There!"

Janet starts to cry, and Kiki pats her gently on her back, then wipes away her tears as gently as she can with a paper towel.

"It's going to be all right," Kiki says. "Don't worry. Now, put on your socks."

While Janet sniffles and puts on her socks, Kiki stuffs Janet's soiled dress and socks into the gift shop plastic bag and ties it closed.

Back on the highway, Kiki pulls off at the very next exit, travels an access road for the next ten miles, doubles back west for another ten miles, then from her window, while moving, accurately tosses the plastic bag into an open municipal trash can. She knows how to hide her tracks, but it's been a while since she's had to employ those skills. Still, she thinks she's done well when she scans the local radio with every passing mile for news of a missing little girl and hears nothing. Radio silence.

During the next day and a half that Kiki and Janet spend together traveling, they exchange very few words. Yet, their silences are remarkably easy, as if this child has already filled that empty place that has gnawed at Kiki for as long as she can remember. That's what she tells herself anyway.

And Kiki spends most of this quiet time making a plan to explain how she left on her vacation alone but returned with an eight-year-old child. Schmuck will need a convincing story, but Kiki is confident she can come up with one.

The first night they stop at a motel called By the Roadside because there is a takeout diner attached and it only costs $35 a night. Kiki wouldn't have stopped at all, but Janet was crying again, and she thought perhaps the little girl was simply exhausted.

When she tucks Janet into bed wearing one of her own T-shirts, she says casually, "You don't look like a Janet to me."

Janet frowns. "I don't?"

"What if you could give yourself a new name? Would you like that?"

Janet shrugs. Not wanting to press too hard, Kiki says, "Well, think about it."

The second night, Kiki is too nervous to stay at another motel, so late in the afternoon, she pulls off at a mall exit, and they go shopping for pillows, sleeping bags and blankets. That night they sleep in the car, Kiki making do in the front seat with Janet laid out in the back.

Kiki wakes early with a stiff neck and gets on the road, anxious to initiate her plans and be back in New Hope before her shift at the golf course. She wants to acclimate Janet to the house so she can feel comfortable leaving her alone while she works out how to deal with everything, tell Schmuck and do some shopping.

She drives for an hour, listening to Janet's gentle snoring before the little girl's head pops up between the seats.

"Good morning, sleepyhead," Kiki says.

Janet rests her cheek on the front seat and blinks.

"What do you want for breakfast?"

Janet once again is surprised to be asked to make such a decision, but after thinking about it for a moment, she says, "IHOP. A Rooty Tooty Fresh and Fruity."

Kiki glances at Janet, whose little cheek is close to resting against her arm. "What's that?"

"I don't know," Janet says. "But I saw it in a commercial. Mom says that kind of food is bad for you, and I'm not allowed to eat whipped cream for breakfast."

"Well, that's ridiculous," Kiki says. "Whipped cream for breakfast is exactly what we need."

Janet sits back and rubs her eyes with both fists, then leans forward and presses her head against Kiki's arm.

"Can I really change my name?"

"Absolutely."

"Madeline," she says. "Like the girl in the book."

Kiki smiles. "Madeline, how would you like a big stack of pancakes covered in whipped cream?"

Chapter 13

Janet, 1992

She is waiting for her mother to come, but she never does. Every day since she came "home" with *her*, after breakfast, Janet goes and sits on the front steps, waiting. *She* doesn't bother her or tell her to come inside, even though today it's raining heavily. *She* simply opens the door and hands Janet an umbrella.

Janet's bum is wet through her new gray coat, to the seat of her new plaid dress. She's also a little hungry. Her stomach grumbles, but she ignores that, has ignored it for days now. She knows that *she* wants her to eat, so she refuses anything except the smallest bite or two of whatever is offered her, leaving the rest untouched. Today was scrambled eggs and buttered toast that *she* cuts up into bite-sized squares. It tastes delicious but Janet stops after two bites of egg and one square of toast. *You don't like it?* She doesn't answer most of the time, but this time she says, "No, I don't like it," and so *she* whisks the plate away with sharp, jerky movements. Janet can tell *she* is angry, so she gets up and silently puts on her coat and goes out to sit on the front steps to wait for her mother.

After a week, Janet is dropping weight and starting to suspect that her mother isn't coming. Still, she waits.

Janet's secret warfare is working. The woman she now thinks of as *Kiki* stops trying to entice her with food and toys and new clothes. She tells her it's time for her to be in school and it's time for Kiki to go back to work. She's short with Janet, doesn't try to kiss her goodnight or hug her good morning. When Janet doesn't answer to being called "Madeline," Kiki stops calling her anything. They sit across the table from each other, Kiki staring off into space, drinking cup after cup of coffee, and Janet staring at the food on her plate, stomach growling loudly enough that they can both hear it.

Janet sits in front of the television, watching daytime soaps and game shows, while Kiki aggressively vacuums. Janet feels Kiki's anger, but she's felt that anger before, and it pleases her that her hunger strike is driving Kiki crazy. She can stand up to Kiki in ways that she could never have with her mother (whose face is becoming harder and harder to visualize, even if she doesn't want to admit it).

The phone rings. Kiki keeps her voice low, but Janet hears her telling somebody she'll be back at work on Monday, *things are getting better, thank you.* Then Kiki moves away from the kitchen door where the phone is hung on the wall, and Janet can't hear what else she's saying. A minute or two later, Kiki hangs up and comes out of the kitchen. She regards Janet from the doorway, then crosses and sits down next to her. Janet watches the opening montage for *All My Children.* She refuses to even look at Kiki.

"We'll go visit the school tomorrow," Kiki says. "Then you'll start on Monday."

Erica Kane is crying on the TV screen.

"Madeline," Kiki says, "I have some...news. About your mother."

Janet looks at Kiki from the corners of her eyes. She holds her breath.

"She's not coming."

For a moment, the only sound is the breathless sobbing of Erica Kane on the television.

Then, Janet leaps to her feet, fists clenched. *Stupid stupid stupid Erica Kane.* She turns, looks at Kiki, then throws herself at Kiki in a ferocious attack, punching, kicking, stomping. She rains blows on Kiki, and Kiki does nothing. Just lets her do it even though it must hurt, Janet making sure to hit/kick/stomp as hard as she can.

When Janet is done, when she understands that Kiki is just going to take whatever she decides to dish out, she stands there, chest heaving, eyes leaking tears to stain the front of her dress (*stupid stupid stupid*), fists tingling.

When Kiki reaches out both hands and pulls Janet to her, clasping her hands around her waist and resting her head against her chest, something (*hope? terror?*) loosens, then lets go, and Janet howls and howls and howls until she's hoarse and choking on snot. Kiki keeps her rooted there, letting her wipe her nose on her shoulder, and eventually, finally, Janet's muscles let go and she feels herself melting into Kiki's embrace (*her body a betrayal, the embrace a trap*).

"I can hear your heart beating, like a little bird."

Janet sighs.

"You're safe now."

Several weeks later, Kiki throws a surprise birthday party for Madeline, who has settled in without any incident at school and already made two girlfriends.

That afternoon, Kiki arranges for the afternoon off and tells both little girls' mothers that they should arrive at the apartment at three thirty. They come with wrapped presents (a paperback edition of *Madeline Goes to Paris* from Katie and a handmade friendship bracelet from Jennifer), and putting her finger to her lips, Kiki ushers them into the living room where Madeline is doing homework in front of the TV, all shouting, "Surprise! Happy Birthday, Madeline!"

Kiki presents jelly sandwiches and a store-bought cake decorated with a big red-and-yellow balloon on a blue string and *Happy Birthday, Madeline* piped in red icing, with ten sparkler candles on it (*nine for each year and one to grow on!*) that Madeline is almost unable to blow all the way out until Kiki leans in and helps her with the last candle.

Everything is going so well. Madeline feels happy, even though she's also a little ashamed of herself for giving into happiness. Katie is funny and really smart, the class clown, even if she's a bit mean. Jennifer is quiet like Madeline and likes to craft. They're the first real friends she's ever had, and she's already been invited to their houses, but Kiki says it's "too soon for that kind of thing." What that means, Madeline isn't sure.

Since the day she'd been told that her mother wasn't coming, Madeline has started every day with a prayer that she's cribbed from Kiki who, after her own daily shower, recites it to her reflection while she moisturizes her face and blow-dries her hair.

God, grant me the serenity to accept the things I cannot change, the courage to change the things I can and the wisdom to know the difference.

The first time she hears Kiki say it, Madeline asks what it means, and Kiki says, "It means we all need to keep trying, every day, to be a better person." And then she says, "I promise I'll never stop trying."

So Madeline's version goes like this: *God, I accept that Mommy isn't coming for me, so please help me try to be like the* real *Madeline.*

After the girls have their cake—chocolate inside with vanilla between the layers (her favorite)—Kiki sets them up to play Madeline's brand-new Monopoly game. She goes over the rules, reading from the inside of the box, while the girls giggle and fiddle with their tokens, itching to just play. At first, it's The Three Musketeers all the way—lots of laughing—but then Katie takes three hundred-dollar bills on one of her turns past Go, and Madeline calls her a cheater, so Katie says, with a sly glance at Kiki reading *Soap Opera Digest* in the chair by the window, "What happened to your *real* mom?"

Kiki lowers the magazine.

Madeline blinks at Katie, turns to look at Kiki, then Jennifer, then back to Katie, and says in a clear, hard voice, "You're a *bitch*."

Katie's eyes narrow, and Jennifer glances nervously at Kiki, who puts her magazine down and stands up. She says, "Adoptive parents *are* real parents, young lady. And Madeline, you mind your Ps and Qs." Then she says, "It's time to go home, girls. Get your things."

Madeline can't believe Kiki has the nerve to act like *she* did anything wrong. Her *real* mother never cared if she used that word; in fact, she always laughed when Madeline said *shit* or *motherfucker*.

When Kiki comes in to say goodnight, she asks Madeline if she's had a good birthday, and Madeline shrugs and says, "Thank you for the gifts" in a way that might as well be *fuck you*.

She lies awake for a long time, waiting. Kiki is a night owl who often stays up late watching the small TV in her room...with the door open. Even after the apartment goes dark, Madeline waits a while longer before getting up to make sure Kiki is asleep. She creeps to the bedroom door, opens it just a crack, mindful of the creak when it's halfway open and slips out the narrow opening into the hallway. She tiptoes down the hall—past Kiki's open doorway—to the living room, through the living room to the kitchen. Her heart is pounding so hard that she has to wait a minute to calm down. Then she very, *very* carefully pulls the step stool Kiki uses to reach the highest shelf in the cupboard over to the phone mounted on the wall. She climbs up the first step and very, *very* quietly lifts the phone off the hook and dials the home number she still remembers.

The phone rings. And rings. And rings. Finally, a groggy voice says, "Hello?" It's not her mother's voice, it's a man. "Hello? Who's this?" groggy and a little angry now.

Madeline hangs up. She descends the step stool, walks over to the sink and vomits up her birthday dinner and the cake and ice cream. It all comes out in a gut-wrenching gush.

The light snaps on and Kiki stands in the doorway, wild-haired, eyes widened in alarm.

"What's happened?" Kiki rushes over, pats Madeline's back gently, using her other hand to push her hair away from her face while Madeline continues to retch. "Oh, honey...." she says.

Then Madeline suddenly twists away and runs out of the kitchen, back down the hall and into the bathroom, slamming the door. She rinses her mouth, gagging a little on the water, spits, rinses again, then sits down on the edge of the bathtub. She can still taste vomit, so she stands up again and brushes her teeth, scraping the brush across her tongue. She looks at herself in the mirror. *God, I accept that Mommy isn't coming for me, please make me brave like the* real *Madeline.* She can hear Kiki in the kitchen, cleaning up her mess, moving the step stool back to its nook. *She was not afraid of mice; she loved winter snow and ice.* Now Kiki's footsteps slowly approach down the hallway and stop outside the bathroom. *Pooh pooh.*

Kiki taps on the door. "Are you okay in there?"

Madeline feels empty, hollowed out. Her stomach clenches.

"Madeline, please answer me. I want to respect your...privacy, but if you don't open this door, I'm coming in."

Madeline gets up and swings the door open, facing Kiki. She says, "Can I call you Mom from now on?"

Kiki looks startled. She nods. "Of course, you can," she says.

Then Madeline walks into Kiki's outstretched arms and holds on.

Chapter 14

Raoul, 1993

He's mad for this guy who's everything he isn't. Tall. *Really* good-looking. A highly educated, highly paid and in-demand surgeon. No roll of flesh around his middle. The exact right amount of body hair. Gary enjoys his adoration, but Raoul understands there's no real hope of them ever sleeping together; they're not even in the same league. They decide to go mini golfing because Gary wants to do something *fun*, and Raoul's idea (seeing *Philadelphia*, the new Tom Hanks and Denzel Washington tearjerker about AIDS) is decidedly not *fun. Who wants to think about that? It's depressing.*

Gary picks Raoul up in his canary-yellow Firebird, and they drive forty-five minutes to New Hope to a place called Schmuck's Mini Golf because Gary thinks it's funny. He's Jewish, from California originally—and not familiar with Pennsylvania surnames apparently—because he pronounces it *schm-uck* instead of *schm-oock.*

"Gonna get us some schmuck at Schmuck's," Gary says nonsensically, but Raoul doesn't correct him. He's just enjoying basking in the glow of Gary's beauty, with the wind in his own (admittedly, thinning) hair on this gorgeous spring day, the fantasy of persuading Gary into his bed so he can show him what's in his heart crowding in every time he lets his guard down.

The woman at the ticket booth is all polite smiles, but Raoul detects that she's picked up their homosexual vibe and maybe she doesn't one hundred percent approve of all that *gaiety.* Gary doesn't care what people think—he flaunts it, pushes their noses into it in ways that Raoul would never dare, having learned (*the hard way*) what it means to be a *queer* in a world where police beat you down, drag you out of your car, arrest you for cruising or public sex, make you lose your job, have to start over.

Gary is already sashaying with purposeful camp toward the chain link gate and the first hole, leaving Raoul to pay the admission. He passes cash to the woman.

"You from around here?" she asks, counting out his change, shoving it toward him.

"Philadelphia," Raoul says.

"Thought so." She grins at him and Raoul realizes she's genuinely friendly, not a threat after all.

"Is this your place?" he asks.

"Oh, no," she says with a laugh. "I'm just the hired help." She points at her name, *KIKI*, embroidered on the front of her bright green polo shirt. "You play golf a lot?"

Raoul laughs and shakes his head.

She seems to want to engage him in conversation, but Gary awaits (impatiently waving a club over his head), so Raoul thanks her again, smiles and hurries after him.

They play all eighteen holes, and, of course, Gary wins. And, of course, he makes it a bet, so Raoul has to pay him twenty bucks at the end, which Gary crows about all the way to the clubhouse where he deigns to purchase the soft drinks since he's the *winner*.

When Gary's pager goes off, he says, "Shit," and fishes it out of his pants pocket, squints at the number, then stands up. "Gotta find a phone," he says.

Gary asks Kiki, the ticket seller at the front, if she has a phone he can use, and she leads them over to the trailer on the other side of the parking lot. Inside, a shrunken old man, wearing a yellowed, formerly white shirt and dusty-looking suspenders, sits at a desk painstakingly entering numbers into an accounting ledger.

"This customer needs to use the phone, Mr. Schmuck," she says loudly, pronouncing the name correctly.

He looks up and waves a vague hand at both her and Gary.

"Go ahead," Kiki says, pointing at a phone on a different desk, then she steps back outside to wait with Raoul while Gary makes his call.

"What's *your* name?" she asks.

"I'm Raoul."

She holds out her hand. "Kiki," she reminds him, and they shake briefly. "I've never met anybody named Raoul before," she says. "Is that Spanish or something?"

"French," he says.

"I like it."

Then Gary comes out, shoving an impatient hand through his thick, chestnut-brown hair, and squeezing himself between them, clatters down the steps in a hurry.

"Gary? What's going on?"

Gary looks up at Raoul, a weaselly smile on his handsome face. "I gotta go.

Emergency. You're going to have to find your own way."

"But—"

"Sorry, buddy. Doctor's life." Then he turns and sprints toward his car, calling over his shoulder, "I'll call you."

Raoul looks at Kiki—he feels suddenly ashamed. He opens his mouth to speak, then closes it again. What can he say? He's been dumped unceremoniously before, more than once. Story of his gay life, wasn't it?

"Where do you live?" Kiki asks.

Raoul sighs. "It's a forty-five minute drive." He feels hopeless.

"I could give you a ride if you wanna wait till after my shift ends." She looks at her cheap elastic band wristwatch. "I'll be done in less than an hour."

"Oh, I couldn't ask you to do that." He turns and walks down the steps. She stays where she is.

"Why not?" she asks.

He looks up at her, then says, "Are you sure?" because, after all, he has no clue how to get home from here—*train? bus?*—and Gary's Firebird has already peeled out of the parking lot. Hitching a ride with this woman seems his safest, cheapest bet.

Her car is a beater Ford Taurus with nonexistent shocks, and she's a terrible driver (causing Raoul to gasp more than once), but Kiki turns out to be a funny, even witty, conversationalist and a lot savvier than he'd given her credit for, judging by her lack of makeup, Schmuck's Mini Golf bright green polo shirt, unfashionable, high-waisted blue jeans and sensible (*admirably immaculate*) Adidas.

It turns out she's a single mom of a nine-and-a-half-year-old, adopted daughter named Madeline and—lucky for him—she has a sitter that night because she wants to see the new Denzel Washington movie because he's her favorite actor.

They bond over their mutual love of Denzel (*our generation's Paul Newman!*), shared birth year (*1954! Me too!*), Utz potato chips (*the* best *potato chips in the whole damn world!*), that Gary's an asshole, and the fact that neither of them are in touch with their families. Her, because she's an only child and her parents are dead (*car crash when she was only sixteen*). Him, because...well, they don't approve of his lifestyle (*thrown out the day after high school graduation when his Republican dad catches him making out with his best friend Rob by the pool at three in the morning.*).

"That's not fair," Kiki says. "You can't help who you are, can you?"

When they get to the city center, Raoul says she can drop him off anywhere, and he can walk from there. When she sees an opening at the curb, she pulls over and jams the brakes.

"Thank you," he says, turning to her, meaning it. "You really saved my ass."

"I was coming into the city anyway," she says.

Raoul starts to get out of the car, then turns back to her. "Wanna get something to eat and then go see the movie together?"

"Why not?" she says.

Chapter 15

Convergence

On the way back to the motel, Leona and Derek don't speak. What is there to say? The uncertain/certain future is a palpable entity, a weight that threatens to smother them both.

They both lie down on the bed, fully dressed, and clasp hands, still not speaking, listening to the water running in the toilet, the low hum of the heater, a car door slam, burst of laughter, a woman's voice calling, *C'mon Roy! Hurry up!*

Derek says, "Let's go get something to eat."

Leona squeezes his hand, and Derek rolls onto his side. He puts his arm across Leona's thinning waist.

"Baby, please tell me what you want me to do."

She shakes her head, dry-eyed. "I'm fine," she says. "Don't worry so much." She pats his hand, then sits up, arranging the pillows behind her, and picks up the TV remote.

While Leona restlessly surfs all six TV stations, Derek gets up and goes into the bathroom. The minute he shuts the door, she drops the remote, grips the bedspread, twisting the fabric in her hands, and bites down on it, using it to stifle silent, agonized screams. When the toilet flushes and Derek comes out, she's back to mindlessly watching the local weather forecast.

He sits down on her side of the bed, facing her, and takes the remote from her hand, aims it at the TV and turns it off. "Talk to me," he says.

Leona's eyes slide toward him, then back at the silent TV. "This was a bad idea," she says.

"I agree. Let's go home."

"No."

"You're not making any sense."

Leona leans her head back, closes her eyes. "Why wouldn't she recognize me?"

"Maybe it's really not her."

"It's her, goddammit," Leona says fiercely, then mimicking Kiki, "*I've been to Niagara Falls many times.* Jesus Christ! I can't fucking *believe* her."

Derek hasn't seen Leona like this in a long time, and he's worried. He wants to say the right thing.

"Honey," he says, taking her hand, "I think we should take Blair's advice, get ourselves a lawyer—"

Leona's shaking her head.

"—make *sure* before we do anything."

Leona brings her head up and gives Derek a hard look—the ghost of the old Leona, out-of-control Leona, reckless, willing-to-wreck-things Leona, the first and only girl he ever fell for, attracted to the flame, always willing to get burned.

"Fuck that," she spits at him. "I haven't got the luxury of time to get this done in the legal system. I fucking know how these things work. Did you forget I spent twenty years watching kids get fucked over by the system? No. That's not happening."

Derek nods, then gets up and goes over to the mini fridge, pulls out an apple juice, cracks it and pours it into one of the plastic cups from the bathroom, hands it to Leona.

"You're supposed to stay hydrated. And you haven't eaten anything since this morning."

He puts on his jacket.

"Where are you going?"

"I'll be back with food so you can take your meds," he says. "We'll eat and make a plan. Okay?"

"Your sister, you say." Raoul holds out his martini glass for a refill. "You never told me you have brothers and sisters."

Kiki takes the glass and pours a solid slug of gin into the shaker. "I divorced my family. I prefer to think of myself as an...orphan. So what?"

"Okay." Raoul studies Kiki's back. "Are you okay with it then?"

Kiki throws a handful of ice into the shaker, measures a shot of vermouth, stirs it ever so slightly with a long-handled spoon before pouring it into Raoul's glass. She turns and hands Raoul his cocktail before she sits, folding her legs under her.

Without taking a sip, Raoul sets the glass down and gin sloshes over the side of the glass. "What aren't you telling me?"

"I was a different person before I met you. I don't like to talk about it because I don't want to think about it. I changed my life. That's what counts." Kiki puts her hand on Raoul's arm. "You and Madeline are my family. The only family I care about."

"Doesn't this mean you'll have to tell her the truth about who she really is? She isn't stupid. She's bound to ask questions." He sips his drink. "I'm surprised she hasn't before now, to be honest."

"*If* it comes up, I'll tell her."

Raoul picks his drink back up, watching Kiki with forced neutrality. "You do you."

"Everything's fine. Drink your drink." She picks up her glass. "To Ezra Miller! Rot in hell!"

Raoul shakes his head, but he clinks with her Perrier and cranberry and drinks to the eternal damnation of his chosen sister's father. *Cheers to dysfunction!*

Madeline hasn't been able to get that odd couple out of her head. The way that woman had stared at her, her wig slightly tipped back revealing shiny, hairless skin. And the guy in a hurry to get her out of there. It felt like something important—a sign? But...of what?

Signs. Signals. Her mother's sudden about-face on her taking over the business.

"What should I do, Keira?" she whispers into Keira's soft ear, the dog's head resting on her shoulder. She's managed to squeeze herself into the too-small space next to Madeline on the couch by half sitting on top of her.

Something about the way Kiki changed her mind is off. Madeline has always been careful not to ask certain questions by mutual, mute agreement with her mother. Some things were better left unexplored. But what's worse is that Madeline's equally sudden decision to break free now seems somehow less exciting than it did two days ago. She's never been much of a planner, has always ridden along with somebody else's plan. That used to drive Jawari crazy.

What do you want for lunch?

What do you want?

I asked you first. Just say what you want.

I don't care.

And on it would go until Jawari finally gave up (irritated) and decided on what they'd have for lunch (sometimes not really what Madeline would want, but at least she knows better than to say that after the fact).

Jawari. She misses her. But Madeline has taught herself well. Missing leads to misery. She prides herself on her ability to let go. Of memory. Feelings. People. When she was a kid, she'd thought of it as her superpower. Life is easier, smoother. Consistency is reassuring, consistency is How to

Get Through. She studied accounting because numbers are consistent, their values unquestionable. Things either added up or they didn't. And if they didn't, there were a limited number of options available to fix it and make the numbers work.

She enjoys her job and loves working with Raoul. Working with her mother can be challenging, but she stands her ground when she needs to, and Kiki will usually back off, listen to her on decisions around expenditures.

Right now, she can't think of any place as cozy and safe as her tiny house, especially with Keira Knightley snoring lightly by her side. So, why would she just blow that up? It seems she is talking herself out of Making Her Big Move.

"What do you think?" she says to Keira.

Her phone buzzes with a text. Raoul. *Are you up?*

Yes.

At your mom's heading over. And he adds 🙂

Madeline texts back 😒

Raoul slips in the door a few moments later. "I don't have long," he says, sitting heavily on the chair across from the coffee table. "How's *your* night?"

"How was *yours*?" Madeline counters.

"I should've stopped at two. Sometimes gin hates me."

Keira ambles over to get some attention from Raoul, resting her head on his knee. "How's she doing?" he asks, stroking the dog's head.

"She seems fine."

"It's hard to believe," Raoul says, scrubbing behind both ears with both hands. Keira's tongue lolls.

"So...." Madeline says.

Raoul puffs up his cheeks, lets out a long sigh. "I shouldn't have come over here." He stands up, pats Keira and goes to the door.

"What the hell, Raoul? What's going on?"

"Ask your mother."

"Ask her what?"

"About your grandfather."

That night, Madeline dreams about the boy with the baseball bat. They're on a Ferris wheel, and as the gondola swings, she sees that there is no safety bar holding them in the seat. She looks over at the boy, but he's not looking at her. He says, *God, grant me the serenity to change what shouldn't be changed* and she thinks, *That's not right.* Then she feels herself sliding off the slick vinyl of the banquette seat and realizes the boy is slowly pushing her forward, and she falls, head-first.

She wakes herself up with a gasp, sits straight up in bed, and Keira Knightley lifts her head, eyes glinting in the half-light of predawn. Madeline's heart pounds sickeningly, so she gets out of bed, pulling the top quilt along with her, to lie down next to Keira on her dog bed, wrapping them both in the quilt. It takes a long time for Madeline's heart rate to return to normal. By then, the sun is up, and it's a new day.

Chapter 16

Aunt Rebekah

It's busy at the course for the first time because it's a Saturday and the temperature soars to eighty degrees. Kiki gets to work late, and Raoul sells the first six tickets to a group of Girl Scouts.

"Sorry," Kiki says, not sounding sorry at all.

Raoul wags his head and steps out of the booth to exchange places with Kiki.

"What's wrong with *you*?" Kiki says, tucking her bag into the corner and lowering the stool to her preferred height.

Raoul just looks at her, lips pressed into a tight line.

"What."

"I've been thinking about it, and you need to do the right thing."

A van pulls into the parking lot, and four little kids pour out of the side door and run toward the ticket booth, trailed by their chaperones, two teenage girls.

"Can we talk about this later?" Kiki says.

Raoul shakes his head and walks away. Kiki sucks her teeth, then turns, smiling, toward her clamoring customers.

"Either of you girls sixteen or under?" she asks the taller of the two.

He loves Kiki, but does he really know her? No, he does not, even after this long. And the last couple of days prove it. If she can lie about being an orphan and lie to Madeline about being adopted, then there's no telling what else she's lying about. Suddenly, Raoul faces the prospect that his best friend—his Friend-Wife, for chrissakes—is a Capital L Liar, and the world he's built the last fifteen years of his life on is sliding off its foundation.

Raoul feels a terrible heaviness as he goes up the stairs. How to face Madeline. She trusts him (he likes to think she trusts him *like a father*). She trusts her mother—the only mother she knows. Are either of them worthy of that at this point? And what does he owe Kiki, if it comes to that? Whose side will he choose when the shit hits the fan? Because for sure, that shit is coming. He swings open the door of the office and stops.

Madeline and a plainly dressed woman with her hair in a low bun sit facing each other on the couch.

"Oh," he says, "excuse me—" He turns to pull the door shut, then turns back, says, "Mads, you okay? You need me to...um...."

"No," Madeline says and looks back at the woman.

Raoul goes out, quietly closing the door behind him. The shit has already started raining down.

"I have other aunts and uncles and—and cousins?" Madeline says.

Rebekah nods, smiles slightly. "We're Amish," she says as if that explains this sudden exponential family growth, then corrects herself, "They are—I'm not. Not anymore."

Madeline blinks at Rebekah (*her aunt*). "What did you say?"

Rebekah stares back at Madeline, then says carefully, "What has your mother told you about us?"

"Nothing. Obviously."

"Oh, goodness." Rebekah looks dismayed. She twists her fingers together in her lap.

"You said you're not Amish...anymore?"

"I never joined the church," Rebekah says.

"And my mother?"

Rebekah shakes her head. "It's not my place to tell you."

Madeline's mouth twists. "Well, you don't think she'll tell me anything, do you? I didn't know you—any of you—existed until today. I don't understand what the big secret is, but it must be something awful."

"It *is* a sad story, Madeline. She had a rough time. She was...different. Not like them. Not even like me. Just different. It's not easy to be *that* where we came from. *Different* scares people."

"You don't need to tell me what it's like to be different," Madeline says. She stands up, needs to move or she'll explode.

Being Amish. Being queer. This woman—her aunt!—doesn't have a goddamn clue.

She goes over to her desk, fiddles with her Mont Blanc pen (a gift from Jawari), her nameplate: *Madeline Morel, Chief Operating Officer.*

Rebekah stands up and smooths the front of her already smooth A-line skirt. She folds her hands together in front of her.

"That man who came in earlier," she says. "Who is he?"

"You mean Raoul?"

Rebekah nods. "What is his relationship to you and my sister?"

"He's my—" Madeline stops. "He's family. Not by blood. But yes, we're a family business." She doesn't know what she's even saying. How to explain the tie that binds Raoul to them and Schmuck's and the entirety of her life?

"And your father? Your real father? Who is he?"

This new aunt is a nosy bitch. Madeline says shortly, "I wouldn't know. I'm adopted."

And now it's Rebekah's turn to be surprised. "Adopted!"

"Yeah," Madeline says, letting the chip on her shoulder show, "...so what?"

Rebekah just says, "Ah," and nods like she knows a secret.

More secrets. Always more it seems.

"I don't know if we'll see each other again," she says, "but I'm glad we had this talk." She reaches into her purse and pulls out a business card, extending it toward Madeline. "In case."

"Okay," Madeline says, taking it ungraciously. "Sure. Whatever."

Rebekah turns and goes out. When she closes the door, Madeline's fingers curl around the card, and she flings it, but it doesn't have any lift, so it just drops to the floor after glancing off Keira's head, startling the dog out of a sound sleep. She looks up at Madeline, reproachful, then bends her head and noses the card.

"I'm sorry, girl," Madeline says. "*You* didn't do anything."

She picks up her aunt's business card—Rebekah Klinedinst, Office Manager, Soleil Chocolate Company with an address in Lehigh—and drops it in the wastebasket.

At closing, Kiki tucks the fat money bag under her arm and locks the ticket booth. A good day, overall. She crosses the parking lot and mounts the steps to the trailer. When she opens the door, the only one inside is Raoul. He's lying on the couch, with his arm over his eyes.

"Well, *that* was exhausting," Raoul says. "Maybe retirement is a good idea after all."

"Where's Madeline?"

He shrugs. "Left twenty minutes ago."

"She say where she was going?"

"Nope."

"Raoul, are you mad at me?"

"Nope."

Kiki walks over and puts the money bag in the side drawer of Madeline's desk, tucking it under some file folders.

"I'm disappointed," Raoul says.

Kiki looks up. "What?"

Raoul sits up. "I said, I'm disappointed. In you."

Kiki's lips draw into a stubborn line.

"I thought we didn't lie to each other," Raoul says.

Kiki sits down at Madeline's desk and rests her chin on her hands. "Okay," she says, "let's have it. Just say what you have to say. I'm sick of this."

"Why do you do it? Why keep something so important from her?"

"Look, I didn't mention my family because they're in the past. I already told you this. I don't want to *think* about them."

"I get it, okay? But you've been promising to tell her for *years* and it's never the right time."

Kiki eyes him, nods. "Oh, that."

"Yeah," Raoul says, incredulous that she can be so cavalier about something so huge. She's having a hard time meeting his gaze.

"What's the point of holding onto this *fiction* that Madeline is adopted? Who does it serve?"

Kiki stares at him with open hostility, and suddenly he understands something he's spent years ignoring, something that's been there all along, hidden beneath the surface of a chosen family that now seems to have been little more than illusion. It's all crumbling.

"What else are you lying about?"

"I don't think we should go there," Kiki says. And then she laughs.

Raoul stands up, nods, his expression frigid, set. "I quit," he says. Then he turns and goes out.

Jawari's sleek black Lexus is parked in the driveway of her tidy brick townhome, shaded by the tender new foliage of twin dogwoods. Madeline parks her VW on the street, then pulls out her phone. She may have deleted Jawari's contact info, but she remembers her phone number.

I'm in front of your place. Got a minute? She waits as the seconds tick by, then sees bouncing bubbles on her screen and finally, *OK.*

Jawari is dressed in sweats and a faded PENN hoodie, and Madeline follows her silently into the kitchen. Cersei the cat is curled up on the window seat, looking out on the small fenced-in yard where daffodils have sprung up across the lawn. Madeline goes over to pet the cat, absently rubbing her under her chin.

"They came up," she says, nodding toward the carpet of flowers outside the window.

Jawari looks up from putting tea bags in cups. "Oh, the daffodils? Yeah. Pretty, huh?"

"Very."

"Gives me an excuse not to mow the lawn too."

She puts a mug of tea on the table, prepared the way Madeline always takes her tea (one sugar and a slug of almond milk), then sits down on the other side and blows lightly across the steaming surface of her own mug.

"What's going on?"

Madeline shakes her head, gives the cat a final chin scratch, then sits down. She curls her hands around the mug of tea.

"I met my aunt today."

Jawari cocks her head. This is unexpected news.

"Yeah," Madeline says, "I know, right? Turns out I have a lot of aunts and uncles and cousins, and apparently a dead grandfather." She laughs. "And they're Amish."

"What the—" Jawari's eyes are round with surprise.

"Well, my aunt Rebekah—that's her name—is not Amish. And Mom isn't Amish. Anymore."

"So, like, they're *shunned* or something?"

Madeline says, "I don't think that's a thing except in the movies."

"What'd your mother say?"

"I haven't talked to her about it."

"Why not?"

Madeline shakes her head, looks down at her untouched cup of tea, takes a sip. *Why not, Madeline? Why not?*

Jawari says, "Are you okay?"

"I have a bad feeling she's hiding—more things. She's acting so weird."

Jawari sits back, folds her arms across her chest.

"I know you think I'm *catastrophizing*—isn't that the word you like to throw at me?—but I'm telling you, there's more she isn't telling me. I think I've always known it."

Jawari sighs. "Just imagine what your life would be like if you didn't always expect the worst."

"It's not *expecting* the worst, it's being *prepared* for it."

Suddenly Jawari bursts into laughter, and then they're both laughing, and it feels good, feels right, feels comfortable. Again. Finally. Jawari was the first girlfriend Madeline had who really seemed to accept her as she is, without trying to change her.

Jawari pulls out an expensive bottle of unopened, imported sake she got as a gift from a work colleague, and they get a little tipsy and talk about how work's going (Jawari's a pharmacist, so business is *booming*) and how Keira's doing (*better than expected*), and then Madeline says she should go, and Jawari says maybe she should stay.

"I'd like to," Madeline says, "but I really have to go home."

"That's too bad," Jawari says.

They get up and Jawari walks Madeline to the door.

"Your birthday's coming up."

Madeline makes a face. "Don't remind me."

Jawari leans in and kisses her. When they pull apart, Madeline says, "What are we doing?"

"Making up?" Jawari suggests.

"What about Sasha?"

"What about her?"

"You two aren't...?"

Jawari shakes her head. "That was a mistake."

"Oh."

"Can we please hit reset?" Jawari puts her hand on Madeline's waist.

"Maybe."

They stand there staring goofily at each other, then Madeline turns to go.

She's halfway across the lawn before she turns, runs back to Jawari still standing in the doorway, kisses her hard and says, "I'll call you tomorrow."

In the car, she puts Jawari's contact info back into Favorites.

Chapter 17

Leona, Alone

Leona watches Derek sleep. He looks like a little boy, his hand curled under his chin, lips slightly open. Such a tender, forgiving man. She'd certainly led him on a miserable chase when they were young, treated him like a comfortable shoe she could put on when the four-inch heels pinched her toes.

It took Janet being kidnapped, then her two years *away* in that hellhole, to understand that Derek was who she needed. It took a couple more years after that to realize that Derek was who she wanted.

She gets up carefully so as not to wake him, goes into the bathroom and eases the door shut. The lights over the mirror reflect off her bare scalp. She paints on two eyebrows, then dons her wig and exchanges her pajama bottoms for a pair of sweatpants.

Back in the room, she pauses to make sure Derek is still asleep, then pulls on a sweater and coat, grabs her cell phone and the car keys and slips out the door, again easing it shut until the lock engages.

In the car, she enters the address into Maps, slides the phone into its holder, and then she's on her way.

The street that Kiki lives on is wide and quiet, with smallish houses, neat yards and soccer mom vans or sensible SUVs parked in driveways. Most of the houses are lit up, and she feels exposed when she pulls in front of Kiki's place, which is completely dark, so she turns off the car and sits in the dark for a few minutes, letting her eyes adjust.

Leona stares at the house. Is that the light of a television flickering intermittently behind the drawn Venetian blinds? She pulls the keys from the ignition and gets out of the car. She looks left, then right, then hurries up the walk to the front door.

Kiki doesn't say anything at first. She just stands there, looking at Leona as if she's dropped onto her doorstep from Mars.

"Can I help you?"

"I'm Leona Lerman. From Niagara Falls. Remember?"

"I don't—who are you?"

"I just told you."

"You were at the golf course today."

"Yes," Leona says. "Can I come in, please?"

"What for?"

"We've met before today. A long time ago."

"I don't know what you're talking about."

"Niagara Falls. 1992."

They lock eyes, then Kiki shrugs, steps aside wordlessly, and Leona moves past her. The curly-haired, brown dog peers at her from an arched doorway, behind which the flickering light emanates, and it *woofs* softly as she approaches.

She feels Kiki's eyes on her back, but she doesn't turn or let it spook her, just leans down and pets the dog, then moves past the dog into the living room, lit only by the television set, now muted, showing an old episode of *Fixer Upper*.

She turns now and faces the other woman, who stands in the doorway, her hand on top of the dog's head. Kiki doesn't say anything, but Leona senses that she's tense, coiled, wary. She needs to be careful of this woman now like she needed to be careful of her then but hadn't realized it.

Kiki crosses to an end table and turns on a lamp. "Can I get you something?" Kiki asks. "Soft drink? Tea?"

"No, thank you."

"Sit down."

But Leona stays where she is, so Kiki sits down on the couch. The dog slowly lowers itself where it is, blocking the doorway.

"What's the dog's name?" Leona asks.

"Keira Knightley."

"That's original."

"My daughter named her," Kiki says. "Now, what's all this about?"

Leona's eyes sparkle with suppressed rage. "You took my child."

Kiki frowns. "What are you talking about?"

"My daughter was taken from a restaurant in 1992. A Chuck E. Cheese. In Niagara Falls. You were there."

"*I* was? I doubt that."

"You were. I knew the minute I saw you again. It was *you*."

"This is crazy."

"Oh, I agree," Leona says.

"You've got me mixed up with somebody else," Kiki insists.

"You said you've been to Niagara Falls lots of times."

"Yeah, but—"

Leona fishes in the pocket of her raincoat and pulls out a folded piece of paper. She holds it out to Kiki, but Kiki keeps her hands at her side, so Leona walks over and flings it at her, then steps back quickly.

With a sour look, Kiki says, "What's this?"

"Take a look."

Kiki sighs, unfolds the paper. She's looking at a photocopy of the identikit drawing of...*herself.* She stares at it, then looks up at Leona.

"It's you, isn't it?"

Kiki looks at the drawing again, shakes her head. "That's not me."

"Yes, it is."

Kiki keeps shaking her head and Leona's hands curl into fists. She wants to scream, *break something, break this* bitch. She says, "You took my Janet."

Kiki stands up. She folds the paper back the way it was and holds it out to Leona, but the other woman puts her hands behind her back. Kiki pastes a sympathetic smile on her face. "This sounds like a very sad story," she says. "I'm sorry I can't help."

"We'll see about that," Leona says. "It'll be easy to prove I'm right."

"Maybe you're so angry because you didn't try hard enough to find...your missing daughter."

"Fuck you," Leona says and takes a step toward Kiki, fists balled.

"I think you should go," Kiki says.

Leona and Kiki stare at each other across the void, and then Leona says, "If you know what's good for you, you'll tell her yourself. And if you don't do it, I will."

Then she stalks past Kiki, ignoring her outstretched hand holding the paper, steps over Keira, who raises her head in surprise, and goes out.

The front door slams, and Kiki lets out a shaky breath. The paper in her hand quivers. She opens it back up, examines the drawing, then goes into the kitchen and lights a match, burning it over the sink, flushing the ashes down the drain.

She's still standing there when the back door opens, and Madeline pokes her head in.

"Good," Madeline says, stepping into the kitchen. "You're up."

Leona has seen Madeline's arrival, watched her get out of her car, walk to Kiki's back door and enter the house. For a moment, she's tempted to go back, but maybe that bitch is telling Janet the truth right now. And maybe Leona is a little afraid of what happens next, of what they'll all do once everybody's in on the secret, when the dust settles. That woman is cool as can be. Outrageous to suggest she didn't look for Janet, yet Leona is sickeningly familiar with the grain of truth contained in those words. *You didn't try hard enough, did you?*

She turns the key in the ignition and pulls away. On the drive back to the motel, she plays some of the possible outcomes like movies in her head. Some of the movies are comedies, some are tearjerkers or horror films, but at the end of each scenario, Janet comes home, settles down in Niagara Falls, and even though they both know they can never rebuild the past, she and Leona eventually become best friends.

But you're dying. So there's no time left, is there?

By the time she pulls into the motel parking lot, her heart is pounding in an uncomfortable way, and she feels sick to her stomach the way she feels after chemo.

Derek is waiting for her, pacing in front of their motel room door, staring down at his cellphone. She parks and turns on her phone, watching him through the windshield. Her phone buzzes and, when she looks, there are at least a dozen texts, each one increasing in panic until the last one: PLEASE PLEASE CALL ME.

He sees her, hurries over and swings open the car door. "Where the fuck have you *been*?"

She's never seen him quite this angry but the look on her face stops him. He crouches next to her, takes her cold hands. "Are you okay? What happened? Where did you go?"

He reaches over and gently wipes her tears away with his thumbs, then he helps her out of the car and into the room because she's too weak and needs to lean on him.

"Where were you?"

Derek hands her a bottle of water and two capsules, her evening meds.

"I went to see *her*."

Derek sits down heavily next to her. "You went to her house? Why?"

Leona shrugs. *Why* is a good question but she doesn't have the answer.

"She denies it," Leona says.

"It," Derek repeats, then, "...the abduction?"

"All of it. She's looking right at that drawing of *her*—right?—and she's like, that isn't me. Such a liar."

"You showed her the identikit? Wow."

"*My* daughter's name is Madeline, she says." Leona punches the bed. "Because *those* were *Janet's* favorite books."

"You told her that?"

Leona shakes her head, not mentioning what else Kiki had said, not wanting to admit that, even to Derek, even now. "I told her we could *prove* it. And that she needs to tell *Madeline* who she really is or I'm doing it."

"I know you're afraid," Derek says.

"I'm *not.*"

They both think about that for a minute, then Derek says, "Are you hungry?"

Leona laughs. "No, but damn, I wish we'd brought those marijuana cookies your sister made me. I could eat one of those..."

"Raoul quit today," Kiki says in this offhand way. An established fact.

"What?" Madeline side-eyes her mother. "*No,* come on."

"He did."

"*Why?* What did you say?"

Kiki shrugs. "I guess he was pissed off about me wanting to sign the business over to you."

"Did *he* say that?"

Kiki shakes her head. "I don't know what he wants. I've been trying to call him all night, but he's not answering."

Madeline's plan of confronting her mother about long-lost *Amish* relations is quickly becoming irrelevant. *Raoul wouldn't just quit.*

"What did you do, Mom?"

"Why is everything always my fault?" Kiki crosses to the refrigerator and pulls out a Perrier and a lime.

"I'm calling him right now. He'll pick up for me."

"No!" Kiki says. "This is between me and him. I don't want you two talking behind my back." She pulls a knife from the drawer and waves it at Madeline. "I mean it. Don't get in the middle of this. If you do, I'll—"

"You'll...what?"

"Just don't."

Madeline takes a deep breath. "This isn't you."

"Oh, it's me all right. We'll just...hire somebody else, show him he's expendable. I'll start looking tomorrow. We'll have to put in extra hours for a while."

Madeline stares at her mother. "He's *family,* not an employee. You need to apologize, take it back. You can't do this to him. To *me.*"

"He did it to himself," Kiki says. "You can't trust him, you know."

"We're talking about Raoul, Mom..."

Kiki shrugs.

"What the fuck happened?"

Kiki sucks her teeth. She hates Madeline's potty mouth.

"This is bullshit."

"Watch your language."

"Fuck you, Kiki," Madeline says.

Kiki viciously slices lime. "Very nice. What a lovely way to speak to your mother."

Madeline whistles sharply for Keira. "Keira, come!" and the dog ambles into the kitchen, blinking sleepily and stretching her back legs, first one, then the other. "Let's go!" Madeline says, impatient now. She opens the kitchen door for Keira who gingerly descends the steps, then turns to her mother.

"You need to call him and apologize. Leave a fucking message if you can't get him to pick up." She pauses to watch Kiki casually pouring herself a glass of Perrier on the rocks. "Mom." Then, "Mom!"

Kiki looks up, her expression bland and unreadable. *Infuriating.*

"Call him."

Kiki waves her hand. "I don't take orders from you, dear."

Unbelievable!

Then, because she can't think of anything better as a comeback, Madeline says, "Aunt Rebekah says you have a sad story. I guess that explains..." her lips twist in disgust, "...your shitty behavior. But it doesn't excuse it."

When Madeline and Keira are gone, Kiki drinks her Perrier in one long guzzle, burps loudly, satisfyingly, then pours the ice cubes into the sink, rinses the glass and puts it in the dishwasher. In the living room, the show is now *House Hunters International* again, so Kiki turns it off. She sits in the dark, one memory chasing another, chasing another, and back again.

No more running.

The chickens have come home to roost.

Ezra is dead.

Raoul is gone.

Soon Janet will be too.

Chapter 18

One Day in the Past

Betty is tucked inside Dawn's coat. She can feel the chicken's feet scrabble for purchase on her undershirt, so she tucks her head to keep Betty from escaping her protection. She knows the chicken is scared, and she doesn't trust that Betty knows she's saving her.

Her shoes sink into thick mud—it only just stopped raining—and her bonnet flaps against her back in a capricious wind that gusts and lifts it, pulling against her throat. She's almost to the Schmidts' farm—*how many miles from home?*—and she prays that the boys won't be in the hay fields on this side of the farm. If they see her, they'll surely want to know where she's going with that chicken.

In truth, she doesn't really know where she's going or what she's going to do with Betty. She just knows that she can't let her father slaughter Betty and force Dawn to eat her, to teach her once and for all: some animals are food, some are workers, but all are under the dominion of man.

She's tired, but she's not giving up. Betty feels so warm, nestled inside her coat, but Dawn's feet are freezing, and her shoes are caked in mud. Her mother will be angry about that. She stops. That's the Schmidts' barn, so she must be close to the main road. What will she do when she gets there? Hitch a ride? *In a car?* She's only been in a car once and that was when the police picked her up after she ran away on Market Day last fall and took her home in their cruiser. That adventure had started out fun but ended up with her father solemnly, regretfully, using a willow switch on her legs that had left stripes on her calves that lasted over a week. She still had a faint mark that looked like a sideways eleven.

No daughter of mine is a thief.
Thou shalt not steal.

But she *was* a thief. If it wasn't nailed down, she'd swipe it. Everybody knew it. The other children—even her siblings—didn't like to play with her because she'd run off with their jacks or their dolls. Whatever they had, she wanted. She couldn't help herself. At the market, she'd been caught stealing everything from crocheted dollies to sticky buns, and once, an entire shoofly pie (wet bottom, her favorite). They'd caught her eating it with her hands in the alley.

The *whoosh* of car tires carries faintly on a bluster of wind, so Dawn picks up the pace. She's close to the road, the path less muddy here. Her shoes really are a mess. Betty shifts her weight again, struggling to turn around, but Dawn holds her tight, whispers soothing words. *Almost there. We're almost there.*

There is a curve in the path ahead where it cuts through a small hill. An apple orchard covers one slope reaching all the way to the tree line, the branches bare and witch-like now, and an electric fence bisects the other and keeps the cows from wandering. No cows now, though. It's almost dark. Everyone is home eating supper.

When Dawn comes around the curve, she stops.

The buggy's reflective bumper winks at her, the sleepy horse, the tall gelding with the one white hoof, stands with his front legs planted, stretching first one hind leg, then the other.

Her father gets out of the buggy, leaving her brothers, Daniel and Peter, sitting in the back seat, and comes toward her.

Dawn backs away. "I'm not coming back!" she shouts. "You can't make me!"

Ezra's expression is mournful (as it usually is). "Get in the buggy, Dawn."

"No."

He walks toward her, and she turns to run but stumbles on a rock. Betty squawks, flapping her wings, then bursts out of Dawn's coat and skitters away as she falls.

Caught.

Punished.

Again.

It's been exactly twenty-seven years, five months, and two days since she had her last drink, and her favorite place to get drunk had always been The El Bar on Front Street in Fishtown. Enough of a dive but also popular enough that she didn't stick out. It was there that she'd met Mr. Arthur Schmuck on a cold and desperate November night, and they'd gotten deliciously drunk together on his generous dime. At last call, when she told him she didn't have any place to sleep, he'd taken her home and installed her in the guest room. She stayed for almost two years before Madeline entered the picture.

They'd been good roomies. He liked having her around because she cooked and cleaned very efficiently and always made him laugh. She didn't care if he was drunk seven days out of seven. In fact, not only were they compatible roommates, they were even better drinking buddies. She didn't tell him about the coke or the weed or the LSD because he would have disapproved, but she never did that in the house, and what he didn't know wouldn't hurt him. He was already half-blind—a real menace on the roads—his hearing was bad, and when he was drunk there was very little that he did notice, but she would never have abused his trust.

At work, it was a different story. He'd told her that right from the start: *We don't drink until after work. That's the rule.* And mostly, she stuck by it, even if he didn't. She quickly picked up the various aspects of running the golf course, and within a few months, she was doing everything except keeping the books, which was strictly his purview and which he locked away at night, sleeping with the key around his neck.

After Madeline came along, and Kiki started AA and stopped being his drinking buddy, Schmuck helped her get her own place. He said he hoped she understood, but *no pitter-patter of little feet for me, hon.* He had even helped her furnish that apartment with some very nice pieces she still had that he got for pennies on the dollar from an antiques dealer he knew in York. He missed her after she moved out, she knew that, but if she had stayed, she might never have quit drinking. That would have been unthinkable while having full responsibility for *a child.*

She and Madeline had lived in that second-floor apartment for the three more years that Arthur Schmuck was alive, before moving back into his brick colonial after he passed. God knows what shenanigans he'd got up to, or if he'd somehow earned it honestly, but when he died and left her everything—including his house and the golf course—there was over two million dollars in his bank account with an additional half a million or so invested in the stock market.

He'd kept her in the dark about his plans, but he had done it right and made her his beneficiary using her new name. He'd been instrumental there as well. Five years previously, when she first came to work for him, she had been forced to confess that Kiki Morel was just a name she'd made up, so he'd gotten her in to see the judge and sign official papers to turn Dawn into Kiki.

Mr. Schmuck had been a drunk, but he had been a good man. He'd treated her like a trusted business partner and loved her like a daughter.

It's early in the day at The El Bar—they've only been open for ten minutes because she's been waiting since before eleven—and the bar smells stale and foreign and comforting and familiar. She orders a mai tai from the bartender, a young woman with white-tipped hair, a stripe of black roots, an elaborate manicure, and a nose ring. *Rooty Tooty Fresh and Frooty. Don't.*

While she waits for her drink, she imagines that Mr. Schmuck is there, sitting on the empty bar stool beside her. They'd toast, and he'd say, *Live a little* or *Life's short and death is long,* and they'd clink and drink.

The bartender puts her mai tai down on top of a napkin and smiles. She's also got a gold cap on one pointy eyetooth. "Running a tab?"

She knows. She can see it.

Kiki nods, the scents of rum and pineapple all around her. She plucks the maraschino cherry from where the bartender has unceremoniously dropped it in the drink and sucks off the sweetness before biting into it.

All you do is lie. Lie. Lie. Lie. Her father's voice in her head. *And you're a thief, the lowest of the low.*

She should go to a meeting, stop this right here, right now, but she picks up the drink and floods her mouth and her senses with the silken flavors of rum and curaçao. *Don't go too fast. You're just getting started.* She puts the drink down and shivers.

She should call Raoul, get him to come fetch her, help her check herself into rehab, but she picks the drink up again and takes another deep swallow. If she's waiting for magic to happen, this buzz isn't it. *Not yet.*

By her third mai tai, she's sick of pineapple juice (it makes her mouth itch), so she orders a mojito instead. The bartender is busy by now with a lunch-time-and-beyond crowd of drinkers, so she doesn't seem invested in cutting Kiki off. *Not yet.*

Four hours later, at five o'clock, when the happy hour drinkers start showing up, Kiki is drunk enough to know that point is coming, so she's got to move on to the next bar on her reunion tour. She settles up, leaving a generous tip. When she slides off the stool, the bartender says, "Want me to call you an Uber?" but Kiki just waves her off with a smile and says, "I'm walking."

She thinks she's steady as she walks out, but she stumbles a little on the raised threshold, and two guys give each other disgusted looks when she elbows into them as they pass by. Then one says, loud enough for anybody to hear, "You better go sleep it off, old lady."

Kiki ignores them both and pulls her purse onto her shoulder, blinking owlishly at the oncoming headlights of Front Street traffic. The cataracts, *baby cataracts,* according to her eye doctor, turn all the lights into angelic haloes. She turns carefully and walks slowly in the direction of Jerry's Bar. In her current state, halfway in the bag, but still feeling powerful (*only lagging a little bit*), she fancies a game of darts and another trip down memory lane with Mr. Schmuck.

Unfortunately, when she arrives, she sees that the place has been completely renovated and is now a *gastropub* full of people that even now she thinks of as "fancy." No amount of travel and money can fully disappear the little girl whose first ride in a car was a police cruiser.

When the snotty, ponytail dude at the podium asks her if she'd like a Table For One, she says dumbly, sadly, "You don't have darts anymore?" and he just stares at her for a moment and says, "Ma'am?" in a way that's more like, *Are you high*? and that makes her giggle. Then he asks her if she'd like him to call her an Uber in a way that's more like, *You're drunk and shouldn't be seen in public,* so she just turns and walks out.

On the street again, she wanders for a while, turning off onto side streets, watching people living their lives inside their apartments and avoiding her on the sidewalks. When she comes to a little park, she sinks onto a bench gratefully. Her knee hurts, and her feet are cold, even though it's still relatively balmy for an April evening.

She takes out her phone, taps in her security code, and opens her Contacts app, then stares at the numbers for so long that the phone times out and she has to reenter her security code. Then she taps her Favorites tab and stares at the only two names there: Raoul and Madeline.

The phone rings and rings and then Raoul's voicemail comes on, so she hangs up and puts the phone back in her pocket. Then the phone rings.

"Why didn't you leave a message?" Raoul says.

Kiki opens her mouth, then closes it. She has no idea what to say. In that extended moment, she and Raoul listen to each other breathing, then Raoul says, "What's wrong?" Then, an ambulance siren wails, and he says warily, "Where are you?"

"I'm doing a reunion tour," Kiki says.

Another long pause. "Are you *drunk*?"

Takes one to know one. "Yes."

"Shit," Raoul says. "*Shit.*"

Kiki laughs. "It's okay" which comes out more like "S'okay."

"What are you doing?"

"Just sitting here. Trying to decide where to go have my next cocktail."

"Why'd you call me then?"

"I wanted to say—" she stops. "I wanted to say you're right."

"Oh, Jesus…" Raoul says, exasperation coming through loud and clear.

"I know…I know. That's what all the drunks say, isn't it? But seriously, you *are* correct. I'm a liar. I've been lying all my life. And I steal things. I'm a stealer of—of things."

"What the fuck, Kiki."

"You and Madeline are so much alike, it's funny, not funny. Haha."

"You need help."

"No, I need—" Kiki stops. "I gotta go."

"Don't hang up—"

And Kiki ends the call. She stares at the phone, says aloud, "What now, Dawn?"

Chapter 19

Monday

Keira Knightley has never—*not one time*—broken house training until today and Madeline is lucky she didn't step in it when she got out of bed at five thirty to go pee. Still, it's shocking and worrisome, and Madeline wonders if it's because of the cancer or because Keira senses how fucked-up everything is. Either way, Madeline doesn't scold her, just cleans it up and takes her outside where, of course, she doesn't take a shit since she's already done that but does manage a few pees on her favorite spots.

Back inside, Madeline feeds Keira (*still a good appetite*), makes tea and toast and listens to the news. Every so often, she goes to the window to see if there are lights on across the lawn, but the house stays dark. She texts Kiki but gets no response, so after she showers and gets dressed, Madeline decides to go over there. She doesn't want to feel this worry about her mother—it isn't fair and it's a burden—but she can't help it.

At the back door, she can see that the kitchen is empty, untouched, so she knocks, calling Kiki's name, and when she doesn't get a response, turns the knob but the door is locked. *Where is she?* Madeline goes around the house and then sees that her mother's car is gone, so she must be at the course, but why wasn't she answering texts?

She can be so obstinate and weird sometimes, and Madeline always feels like she ought to be used to it by now, but if she's being honest, she isn't used to it, doesn't want to become used to it. Her mother needs to grow up, stop living in a fantasy world, and she definitely—*definitely*—better be making up with Raoul at this very moment. Madeline feels ready—*this time no holding back*—to tell her mother some hard truths and demand some in return.

She doesn't know why she decides to do it, but when she goes back inside at her place, she gets the spare key to Kiki's and, with a quick *stay here* to Keira, recrosses the lawn, and before she can second-guess the wisdom of doing it, inserts the key and goes inside.

The house feels as empty and the air as stale as if Kiki had been gone for a month, yet everything looks just as it always does: tidy, dust-free, vacuumed and polished. Kiki's obsession with cleanliness is legendary. No one is allowed to even put dishes in the dishwasher because they don't do it right, at least not the way she does it.

Madeline moves through the kitchen into the hallway, glances into the living room where her own image stares back at her from every surface, then slowly climbs the stairs. It's been a while since she was upstairs, the last time being two winters ago when Kiki came down with a terrible case of bronchitis and needed nursing for several days. She'd slept in the guest room and had spent her days bringing her mother soup and tea and sitting on the easy chair in her mother's bedroom watching television with her or reading or surfing the internet while Kiki slept.

Without really understanding why, Madeline feels uneasy confronted by the two closed bedroom doors on either side of the bathroom. The bathroom door stands ajar and there's a sour-smelling towel crumpled in the middle of the floor which she picks up and puts into the hamper. When she comes out, there's a moment when she thinks: *forget it, go home*, but her feet have another idea, and she's turning the knob to her mother's bedroom before she can effectively talk herself out of doing it.

The tableau that greets Madeline elicits a shocked intake of breath.

The room is in shambles, as if every drawer has been emptied and the items tossed in the air to land wherever. Heaps of clothes and shoes, piles of jewelry, handbags and scarves, bras and slips and undies cover every surface. A whirlwind visited the room and left this mess in its wake. Madeline shuffles through the mess, almost tripping over a Manolo Blahnik gold stiletto (she knows what it is by its red sole) and snagging a heavy, intricately carved, gold chain (real *gold?*) on the toe of her loafer. She had no idea her mother favored four-inch stilettos or gold necklaces.

She starts to register something swirling beneath the surface of what she sees as she turns slowly, taking in the chaos. Shoving aside a pile of cashmere sweaters in a rainbow of colors, Madeline sits heavily on the bed, her hand absently stroking the softness. She picks up a creamy beige sweater, its tag still attached, and it hits her. These items have never been worn—they all still bear their expensive price tags or the sheen of newness, and Madeline doesn't recognize any of this stuff as anything that her mother has ever worn. Not once.

She springs to her feet and pulls open her mother's closet door. Neat piles of folded sweaters and tops, dresses, pants and skirts on hangers, her mother's favorite pair of patent leather dress flats lined up next to her winter boots and extra sneakers. Everything familiar. Madeline stares at the clothes, then turns back to the room.

There. Under the bed, peeking out from under the old-fashioned flounce, the corner of a white box. Madeline kneels on a pile of lacy underthings she'd never imagine her mother would wear and pulls out the flat-lidded box. Inside are papers. On top is a deed to the house (mentioning Mr. Arthur Schmuck), then some papers related to what Madeline realizes are a series of loans on the equity of the house, all of them marked paid in full. Here is the bulky envelope containing the papers her mother tried to force on her the other night and next is a flat manila envelope, the tape long ago having lost its stick and the clasp missing both metal prongs. She pulls out that envelope and peers inside, pulling out a piece of paper.

It's a copy of her birth certificate? She's seen this before. The name of the mother who'd abandoned her and then had the grace to die in a drowning incident. *Dawn Fisher.* A woman about whom she feels nothing.

She goes back into the envelope and pulls out several pages folded into quarters. She unfolds the pages, smooths them out. It's another copy of her birth certificate, except, *that's not right.* Madeline's brain is having a hard time processing what she's seeing. In the space for the mother's name, on this birth certificate, it says *Janet Fisher.* She stares at the name.

All of the four folded sheets are versions of her birth certificate with a different first name for the mother and the same last name, Fisher.

Madeline breathes in and out slowly, measuring her breath because she's suddenly breathless. She turns back to the box. A piece of plain cardboard. Underneath are two things. One is a newspaper clipping from 1992. The headline reads: Missing child in Niagara Falls. The short article offers few details, only that a woman named Leona Albright reported her child missing from the Chuck E. Cheese on Niagara Mall Boulevard.

The other thing is a flattened mesh...hat? No. Madeline pulls the bonnet back into shape. It's one of those mesh head coverings Amish women wear. In faint handwritten letters on the inside band is written the name: *Dawn.*

Raoul hasn't seen five thirty in the morning since he waited tables at that breakfast joint in the Gayborhood back in the early aughts. He's forgotten how lovely it is to drink coffee while the sun rises. Who knew what kind of hours he'd need to keep now that he was unemployed.

Was he unemployed? (*Did he want to be unemployed?*)

It's not like he has any savings to fall back on. Saving isn't Raoul. Spending is Raoul. And spending is Raoul and Kiki together, too. So many hours spent at Boyd's and Neiman's and Saks. They both adore Saks! Of course, Kiki is much thriftier than he is. She'll try on, sure. But she rarely buys. At least not for herself. And many times, they get home and something he's really wanted but has decided he can't afford appears and drops in his lap. A queen bestowing gifts upon her loyal friend and confidant.

They swan around all winter because they work their asses off all summer and fall to make bank.

And the vacations. Paris one year. The Bahamas the next. Barcelona after that. Kiki was always hell-bent to ensure that Madeline got exposed to the good things in life, to learn to recognize quality.

He'd been invited when, in the July that Kiki turned fifty, she decided they should visit Austin, Texas, because she had miles, and they could all three fly first-class and stay in a Hilton almost for free. But he didn't get invited every time. And that was fine. Those times, he'd take himself to Provincetown or Fire Island, and one year, he and Gary took a very exciting (if dangerous) trip to Istanbul. That was the last time he'd seen Gary, in fact. Where was Gary now? Dead? Married? Still chasing.

He needs to call Madeline, find a way to tell her about Kiki. They'll make a plan, go rescue her from whatever shit she's landed in, patch things up and make amends. Or is he just kidding himself? Maybe this is it. The end of an era. He's always known you only got in so far with Kiki before the shutters came down. And that had always been okay. He hadn't been any more willing to revisit his past than she was hers.

But he despises lying. And he despises himself for not even recognizing it as lying, instead consistently attributing it to past traumas better left uncovered.

His phone rings, and when he answers, Madeline says, "You need to come over here. Right now."

Madeline is sitting on the front steps with Keira at her feet, when Raoul pulls up. Keira wiggles over to Raoul and he pats her absently, noting that Madeline looks pale...and stressed. Keira looks from him to Madeline and back again trying to understand why her people aren't giving her more attention. Her tongue lolls.

"What's going on?"

"Mom's gone. Have you heard from her?"

Raoul hesitates, lifts his shoulders, noncommittal. *He hates lying, doesn't he? Why not just tell her now?*

Madeline sighs, then stands up. "Come inside. I have to show you something."

The house still retains its air of abandonment. Madeline tells Keira to *Wait!* then starts up the stairs. Raoul stays at the bottom, his hand on the railing, paused. At the top, she turns, "It's up here."

Reluctantly, Raoul follows and finds Madeline waiting outside Kiki's closed bedroom door. She swings it open and ushers him inside.

Both of them stand there for a minute, Madeline allowing Raoul to take it all in, and Raoul staring, uncomprehending, at the mess.

"What is all this?"

Madeline picks up the creamy cashmere sweater and holds it out in front of her. "Everything still has the price tags on it," she says. "Everything."

She leans down and picks up the gold chain. A tiny tag dangles from the clasp. "This cost twenty-five hundred dollars." She crosses the room and picks up a tangle of bras. "These aren't even her size." She drops the bras and gathers a pile of party dresses heaped on the bed. "Neither are these." She throws them back where she got them.

Raoul is trying to grasp an important thought that refuses to form itself.

Madeline says, "There's more." Then she turns and goes out of the room, and Raoul hears her going downstairs.

He looks around at the loot. *The loot.* His thoughts crystallize, roll out like endless ticker tape to be interpreted, and his breath catches in his throat. *We adore Saks!*

Downstairs, he joins Madeline and Keira in the kitchen, sitting heavily in a chair at the table. Madeline stands at the window with her arms crossed over her chest. They look at each other for a long moment, then Madeline says, "Look in the envelope."

Raoul reaches for the manila envelope in the center of the table. When he's finished paging through each of the papers, he spreads them all out on the table in front of him and looks up at her.

"Mads..."

"What does it mean?"

"I don't know," Raoul says truthfully.

Madeline unfolds her arms, and Raoul sees she's holding something white. She tosses the bonnet onto the table. "Look on the inside band."

Raoul turns the bonnet over and picks it up. The name *Dawn* printed in a child's hand, in indelible ink, faint but visible.

"Who is *Dawn*?"

Raoul returns Madeline's gaze. "Don't look at me like that. I've no idea."

"You don't know anything about this."

"No," Raoul says, perhaps a bit defensive.

Silence stretches after that. Finally, Madeline says, "I need to track her down. Will you help me?"

"I think she's somewhere in the city. When she called—" he stops. "I'm sorry. I should have said. I just—" *No excuses. Buck up, buckaroo.* "I think she's drinking."

Kiki hopes Madeline hasn't had a chance to make the previous day's deposit. She needs cash if she hopes to remain untraceable.

Fueled by a pot of coffee and chain-smoking half a pack of Marlboro Lights she'd picked up somewhere the night before, Kiki drives slowly toward the golf course. If either of their cars is there, she'll take off. If not, she's in like Flynn.

No cars. She swerves into the parking lot.

In the office, she goes directly to Madeline's desk. The drawer where the money bag is kept is locked, of course, but they all know where Madeline hides the key, and when she opens the drawer, thankfully, the money bag stuffed with bills is still there. She shoves the paper money into her pocket, zips the bag of change back up and puts it back in place, locks the drawer and re-hides the key.

At the door, she turns back. The trailer walls are covered in framed photos of the three of them, playing golf, installing the Rex in 2005, handing out trophies at their yearly Labor Day tournament. When Mr. Schmuck was alive, the walls were bare except for his Playboy calendar and a dart board.

Raoul's desk is a mess (like always), except—Kiki frowns. In the middle of his desk blotter is an envelope, the clutter around it swept aside so it stands out. She knows she should just get out—they could walk in any minute—but she can't resist seeing what it is.

The name on the envelope is hers. She sweeps the envelope up and hurries out, locking the trailer door behind her and half-running to her car.

She pulls into a gas station near the interstate for gas which she can now safely pay for with cash and while she's waiting for the tank to fill, she looks over at the envelope, toys with it for a minute, then picks it up and pulls out the single sheet of folded paper.

Kiki,

I'm sorry about your dad. I'm sorry too that you don't trust me enough to be honest with me. I wish you did. We said some pretty ugly things to each other, but I hope we can come back from it. Maybe someday. For now, I want you to know that I love you and

Madeline and Keira Knightley. I'm here for you all even if I'm not here anymore.

> *Love,*
> *R*

Kiki stifles a sob. A tap on the window makes her jump. The irritated face of a young man through the glass. He points toward his truck idling behind her.

"Are you *done*? I'd like to get some gas, lady."

She puts the car into gear and pulls away from the pump, then pulls in next to the curb and turns the car off. Her hands are shaking.

Her phone buzzes. *Where are you? Please text me back, Mom. We need to talk.*

Kiki turns the car on and pulls away from the curb. She needs a drink.

When Leona and Derek arrive at Schmuck's promptly at eleven thirty (opening time), they're surprised that it's deserted and, evidently, unexpectedly closed for the day.

"What now?" Derek says.

"Go to her house," Leona says.

So they drive to Kiki's house, but when they get there, that too is deserted. No cars. No dog. No signs of life either in the main house or the tiny house in the back.

"And now what?" Derek says.

Leona stares out the side window, then turns to Derek. "We could try to break in."

Derek laughs.

"I'm serious."

"No, Leona."

She shrugs. "Okay, then let's go back to the motel and have sex."

Chapter 20

Falling

She's moved on to bars with names like Dirty Joe's, The Dead End and Tin Roof Tavern that have a buck fifty PBR's and three buck well drinks. Today is vodka day starting with Cape Cods, progressing through dirty martinis (*easy on the vermouth*) and ending with shots. Even though these are not the types of bars that attract happy hour yuppies or slumming hipsters, she likes to stop drinking around five so she has time to sober up before driving to whichever fifteen-dollar-a-room motel on Route 30 she chooses that night to crash.

Tonight, however, she stays on that vodka train until well past eight and barely makes it to the tragic women's bathroom in time before letting loose, flushing away the last two hours of good alcohol. *Oh, well.*

She does feel better afterward, but she looks a mess. She washes the ends of her vomited-on hair in the filthy sink and, while she's drying it under the hand dryer, remembers another bathroom and a woeful little girl in a sad, makeshift, bright orange tutu. Remembers the constant refrain running through her head as she drove through the night to get across the New York state line as quickly as possible, wheels spinning toward home: *Thou shalt not steal thou shalt not steal thou shalt not steal.*

When she comes out of the bathroom, Kiki decides she deserves one more drink for the road, and while she's nursing that Russian vodka on the rocks, decides she'll spend the night not in some godawful motel, but on her much comfier office couch. *Why not?* She'll be out of there first thing in the morning, and they'll never even know she's been back.

She's not quite prepared for the darkness of the roads after she exits the highway, so she drives extra slowly, much to the annoyance of the cars trapped behind her on the two-lane, hedge-lined road. She holds her breath each time another car comes at her head-on, squinting against the oncoming dazzle of headlights.

But finally, she arrives. She doesn't park in the front lot but turns onto the dirt service road and parks around back, between the trailer and the propane tank. It's dark as hell, but she uses her phone flashlight and when she's finally inside the pitch-dark trailer, door locked behind her, she plugs in her phone on Madeline's jack, takes off her glasses, sinks down onto the couch and, pulling her smoke-stinking blazer around her, falls immediately to sleep.

She wakes with a start. *What was that noise?* Inside the trailer, her eyes adjusted to the dark, she can see shapes. She fumbles for her glasses. Another *thump* followed by a loud *crash.*

Kiki is on her feet before she realizes she got up. Her heart thuds, a sickening rhythm in her chest. She reaches for her phone. 2:17 a.m.

CRASH!

Looking around for a weapon, she sees the baseball bat standing on its business end in the corner, the bat that Madeline and Raoul took off that vandal. She picks it up, weighs in her hand the solid wood.

Outside, the moon provides enough light for her to see across to the golf course, but on first scan, she doesn't see anything. *There!* A shadow moves inside the clubhouse, followed by another loud crash and the sound of shattering glass.

She walk-runs toward the latched service gate next to *Hole #6—A Skunk's Tale*, opening the gate as quietly as she can, then circles around the now-still spiral obstruction, the tips of those white tails gleaming in the moonlight, and comes around the back of the clubhouse. She hears grunting—*somebody moving something heavy?*—and reaches into her pocket. *Her phone is still plugged in, back in the office.*

Holding the bat with both hands, she squares her shoulders and steps around the winged sides of the clubhouse. Inside, the shadow (a man) rocks the soda vending machine he's pulled away from the wall in an attempt to tip it over.

"Hey!"

The shadow stops rocking the machine, straightens up.

"Get out of here," Kiki says.

The shadow comes toward her, and she backs away, holding the bat in front of her.

The kid emerging from the darkness of the clubhouse can't be more than fifteen years old. Skinny. White. With a constellation of pimples across his forehead and lank hair that falls to one (shaved) side of his head. A black hoodie and jeans hitched below his boxers.

He assesses Kiki, the bat, and says, "That's mine."

"You're trespassing. I'm calling the police."

The kid shrugs then, without warning, turns away from her and lopes off, zigzagging among the course obstacles. He calls out, "I'll be back, bitch…" A threat and a promise.

It takes several minutes for Kiki's heart rate to return to normal, then she enters the clubhouse and switches on the wall lights. Broken glass, bars of candy and packages of Tasty Kakes strewn everywhere from the smaller vending machine turned on its side, which explained the crash she'd heard. Lucky he didn't get a chance to trash the big soda machine. That would have been a real mess. But clearly, it was time to spend some money to install that new fence and hire overnight security.

It feels both comforting and strange to be thinking about golf course business at this moment.

Back in the trailer, it takes Kiki an hour to get back to sleep because she can't stop thinking that she's actually very lucky the boy didn't attack her, push her down…or worse. She pictures telling Madeline and Raoul about the incident and them being amazed at her bravery.

Finally, she gets up and unplugs her phone so she can turn on her Calm app. She sets it to Tropical Ocean Sunset.

She dreams that she's playing golf with Raoul and they're both using baseball bats instead of clubs, but somehow they're both excited about this "new way" of playing. At some point, Raoul is gone and she's playing by herself, and she knows she's gone way over par, but she also knows it's only because the baseball bat makes a very poor putter. She notices that a small crowd has gathered, waiting for her to finish the hole. Suddenly, Leona is standing next to her and saying, "You suck at this worse than I do," and Kiki knows Leona is referring to her mothering skills, but Kiki keeps hitting the ball with the bat and missing the cup.

The phone on her chest is vibrating. Kiki brings it close to her face.

Unknown caller. 7:47 a.m.

Kiki sits up, heart pounding. She stands too quickly and has to sit down again because her head is spinning. She has a terrible metallic taste in her mouth, as if she's bitten her tongue and drawn blood, and she's simultaneously thirsty and nauseated. She tries some deep breathing but that only makes her more anxious. She pushes herself up and goes into the bathroom.

She rinses her mouth, then has a pee. She avoids looking in the mirror until she's combed her hair. Even then, the way she looks is shameful. She doesn't have a change of clothes, but she has an emergency pair of clean underpants in her desk drawer, and she exchanges her filthy, droopy blazer for her SCHMUCK'S MINI GOLF branded rain jacket hanging in the closet. She debates taking Madeline's cardigan from the back of her desk chair, then decides against it.

Hopefully they won't even know she was here.

How long is she going to run?

A little while longer.

And she likes having a safe place to sleep.

Leona is coming up the steps with Derek on her heels when Kiki opens the door. Everyone freezes.

Derek says, "Hello, there."

Leona says, "I have cancer."

Kiki says, "I was just on my way out."

The silence that follows this non-conversation lengthens until Derek says, "We need to talk," which galvanizes Kiki. She says, "Not now." Then she takes a step forward, and another, forcing Leona to retreat back down the steps, and when they're all clustered at the bottom of the steps, Kiki says, "I'm sorry, but I need to be somewhere."

Leona says, "Do you think you're in charge here? I could have you arrested right now."

Derek adds, "But we don't want to do that, do we, honey?"

Leona slaps his mouth shut with a look. "That girl you call Madeline is my Janet. You're the one who took her. Okay? Right?"

Kiki keeps her mouth shut.

"I told you to tell her the truth. Did you do that?"

Kiki turns to walk away, and Leona grabs her by the arm, sinking her fingers into Kiki's upper arm flesh.

"Let me go," Kiki says quietly.

"Honey, let her go."

Leona not only holds on, but she steps in closer. "In the old days, I would've knocked your sorry old ass to the ground." She lets Kiki go, shoving her a little in the process, then takes a step back. "Before you go, answer me one thing."

Kiki nods, once.

"Why'd you do it? Why *me*?"

Kiki looks at Derek, then back at Leona. "Why *you*? It wasn't about *you*. It was about that little girl, left there like that while *you* whined about how annoying and *gross* she was. I *saved* her from you."

Derek puts his hand on Leona's arm.

"I changed my life for that child," Kiki says. "*I'm* her mother."

Leona is flushed all the way down her neck, but her voice is quiet and calm. "No," she says, "you're a kidnapper."

Kiki shakes her head and walks away. She doesn't look at them, still standing there when she backs out, doesn't even glance in the rearview mirror.

Derek calls Dr. Sarris from the parking lot. The emotional storm that followed the confrontation with Kiki has taken its toll and he hopes Leona will sleep for a while. The doctor is concerned, but even though Derek hints around that he would like her to recommend they return home immediately, Sarris brushes that off and tells Derek she thinks this *whole situation* needs to be resolved, that Leona's well-being depends on her being able to resolve the central mystery of her life before her life ends.

After that, Derek goes for a walk and winds up at a little bar with a TV set showing the Phillies' home game and a boisterous group of college kids playing pool. He sits at a table by himself at the back where he can observe and drink his Bud draft without having to engage with anybody. Observer status is his jam.

When he gets back to the motel, Leona is awake, dressed and wearing her wig. They watch TV for a while—local news and weather—then Derek goes out at five thirty and picks up Chinese takeout that they eat in bed, watching *Jeopardy*.

"Do you think I was a terrible mother?"

Derek finishes his bite of moo shu, wipes his fingers on his paper napkin, then mutes the TV and turns to Leona. "Of course not."

"Maybe I was."

"Leona..."

"No, seriously, maybe Janet *was* better off with that woman."

Derek says, "Stop. That's ridiculous. She's clearly..." Derek searches for the right word. "She's not right in her head. To do that, you'd have to be some kind of crazy." He takes her hand. "I know you don't like how people throw that word around, but it's true."

Leona says, "I've been thinking about it all day. What she said. I think it's true. That day, I was mad at Janet for not fighting back, letting those little boys hurt her like that. I was trying to be nice by taking her to lunch but—" she stops. "But when she threw up, I just...couldn't *deal* with it and I left her there." She looks at Derek. "It's just like she said. I left her there."

"Listen to me. You didn't leave Janet in the woods. You went to the bathroom. You couldn't have known some—some *psycho* would snatch her."

"She's not psycho, Derek," Leona says. "And Janet *is* her daughter. Isn't she?" She picks up Derek's hand and kisses it. "I'm okay, you know."

"I know you are," he says, even though he doesn't know that at all.

"She really isn't *my* Janet. She's...herself at this point, isn't she?"

"Yep."

"Maybe she'd be better off not knowing."

"It's your decision."

Leona swings her legs off the bed and stands up, stretching and rolling her neck. She says, "I'm sick of this room. Let's go do something."

Whenever Madeline has said she doesn't remember her childhood, her mother has met that declaration with sympathetic clucks or blithe dismissals. Her sole memory of any time before she was in middle school is of two little boys ambushing her on her way home from school and pushing her around, then hitting her in the stomach with books.

These flashes of memory are vivid (*a strange grassy lane*) but disjointed, bracketed by blackness and a helpless, visceral fear. How they left her, how she eventually made it home, and what consequences those boys either suffered or avoided in the aftermath are gone from her memory, if she ever knew to begin with. She'd learned over time not to talk about that incident with Kiki, who consistently denied it ever happened whenever she brought it up, because her mother's flat denial punches her with the same sickening thud as her memory of those hits.

She can't figure out any of this *fucking mystery* without Kiki but, realistically, she knows better than to expect that her mother will volunteer the answers. Kiki's gone AWOL anyway. And since, to her surprise, Raoul is as in the dark as she is, she can only think of one person who might give them a clue: her newfound Auntie Rebekah.

After Raoul leaves, she feeds Keira and texts Jawari. *What's up, buttercup?*

Hey! Just got home from work with a bottle of wine…?

Have to stop at work first—see you in 30?

Perf

When Madeline goes inside the trailer, she knows immediately that someone—her mother, of course—has been there because all of Raoul's untidy desk piles have been shoved aside. Had she been looking for something? And, of course, no note or explanations. Sneaking around like a thief. *Like a thief. My mother is a criminal.* This thought so disturbs her that, for a moment, Madeline wishes she could go back in time, never have gone upstairs or looked inside her mother's bedroom. She'd invaded her mother's private, fucked-up world, and now that fucked-up-ness was coming back onto *her.* It was starting to feel like the buildup to something really bad, something maybe none of them would be able to come back from.

Still, she crosses to her wastebasket and paws through the dirty tissues, pencil shavings and candy wrappers until she finds the crumpled business card with her aunt's phone number.

"Hello, Madeline," her aunt says in that same, calm voice. "I'm glad you called."

Madeline explains that her mother isn't well and that they're worried she might be in trouble. Fortunately, she doesn't have to go into detail because Rebekah quickly agrees to meet her. They arrange to each drive halfway, first thing in the morning, and Rebekah suggests they meet at the Nockamixon Falls overlook, a pull-off on Park Road, just west of the town of Ottsville.

When Madeline hangs up, she sits at her desk for a moment, then texts Jawari. *Can you come to mine? Don't want to leave Keira alone for too long* 🖤 She waits, watching the bubbles, then *k see you in 10 bringing wine you better be thirsty* 😬

Maybe one good thing will come out of this. Maybe what she's needed to do all along is reach out, open up, grab what she wants. *Is this what people call optimism?*

Before she leaves, she posts an update to Schmuck's Facebook page that says, "Due to unforeseen circumstances, we'll be closed until Monday! Sorry for the inconvenience!" Then she decides to grab the money bag to make sure the deposit gets in first thing Monday morning.

But when she pulls the bag out, she realizes without even having to look that the bills are missing. Did Kiki take the cash when she was here? *Of course she did.* Madeline checks the hiding spot for the spare key and puts it in her pocket when she leaves. If her mother was going to be this way, then she needed to take steps to protect all of them. God only knew how she'd account for the missing receipts on the books.

While she's walking to her car, her phone dings.

How's Keira?

Her mother. Madeline stares at her phone, then taps a message. *Did you take the money from the bag?*

Bubbles, then...nothing further. This was getting ridiculous.

Much later, after the wine, cozied up in bed with Keira draped across the end and both of them with their toes jammed under her warm body, Jawari says, apropos of nothing, "I feel sorry for your mom."

Madeline turns her head to look at her. "Wow. That's a surprise."

"I know. But listen, obviously, she's got a lot of issues."

Madeline has told Jawari about the multiple birth certificates—they've already thrown around dozens of theories about what that meant with no conclusions drawn—but she still hasn't told her about the *stolen loot* in her mother's bedroom. What would Jawari say then, if she knew?

"Pfft." Madeline sits up, adjusts pillows behind her, fussing because she's starting to feel...fussy. "Mom's just acting like a jerk, abandoning her responsibilities and jeopardizing how many years of sobriety? That's just stupid." She folds her arms across her chest. "I've never seen my mother take a drink. Ever."

"Exactly!" Jawari says. "And I'm just saying it seems like she's in a bad way. Maybe she doesn't want you to know where you came from because she doesn't want you to be hurt by it. You said yourself you guys didn't talk about that. Like it wasn't allowed."

Madeline sighs and reaches forward, coaxing Keira to come between them, then cuddles with her. Keira pants excitedly, looking from her to Jawari and back.

"It's weird...when I was young, I knew not to ask about it. And when I got older, I just wanted to live my life forward, not backward. I'd let all those questions go by the time I was a teenager."

"Well," Jawari says, then yawns, "I hope she'll be okay."

"Me too," Madeline says but keeps her doubts about that to herself.

At some point, they fall asleep on top of the covers, then Keira wakes them up by jumping down off the bed, and after that they make love again, and after that they get properly into bed, under the covers.

Madeline lies awake for a long time after Jawari falls asleep. She tries to recall the moment when she gave up wanting to know where she'd come from, but that moment is impossible to pinpoint. One day she had simply stopped thinking about it. And never thought about it after that. Because that's how she has learned to deal with things she knows she can't change.

Looking at it squarely, outside of her own obvious biases, it was clear: Jawari was right. Her mother is a good person who has some issues, like they all do. On the one hand, she is the soul of law-abiding and rule-following. She stops completely at stop signs, sneezes into her elbow, obeys the written and unwritten rules in every way. She'd become a hard-working, successful businesswoman—without a high school diploma—who'd taken what she'd been given and turned it into a going concern. She was a loving mother who'd given her daughter everything she'd never had. And she was a caring (though not always 100 percent supportive) friend to Raoul. But. But the inescapable truth was that Kiki was also possibly a lot of other not-so-good things. *Thief. Liar. Drunk.* And right now, Madeline's best hope of finding out how these two Kikis could coexist in the same person she's known her whole life is going to be when she meets her aunt in only a few, short hours from now.

Chapter 21

Nockamixon

Keira Knightley loves a road trip, and Madeline has to admit the scenery on the way to her rendezvous is, in a word, gorgeous. She feels a bit guilty closing the course on a weekend forecast of balmy temps, with the sun shining, and with people out and about looking for fun, but fortunately, her guilt is overcome by her *need to know* and she's counting on Aunt Rebekah to fill in some blanks.

What she hasn't counted on is seeing her aunt waiting by a silver-blue Toyota accompanied by another, much older woman, whom she introduces, simply, as Sarah. Sarah is short and leans on a cane. In contrast to Rebekah's gray cloth coat, she wears an expensive-looking camel hair coat belted around her comfortable middle. They each greet her and Keira warmly, with soft handshakes for her and head pats for the dog.

Together, they all walk down a leaf-littered path facing the falls, Keira sniffing this unfamiliar place with great enthusiasm. The water cascading toward them, over the manmade steps of the spillway from Nockamixon Lake above, is a springtime gush of raw, noisy power.

Rebekah has to raise her voice to be heard over the rushing water. "Sarah knew your mother. I thought she might be able to help."

Madeline nods, then pulls the crumpled bonnet from her jacket pocket and hands it to Rebekah who turns it in her hands. "Look inside," Madeline says.

"I know what it says."

"Who is she?"

Rebekah does a perfect head tilt. "Where did you get this?"

Madeline flushes. "I found it in a box of…" she hesitates, "…things under my mother's bed."

"I thought you knew. Dawn was her name—Kiki's name. Before." Rebekah looks for help from Sarah, but Sarah suddenly looks like she'd rather be anywhere but here and won't make eye contact with either of them.

Madeline shakes her head. "But the name of my biological mother—the one on my birth certificate is Dawn. Dawn Fisher. She drowned when I was eight." She looks helplessly at Rebekah. "I desperately don't understand any of this."

"Well...Dawn...I mean, your mother, she wouldn't have been able to—to get pregnant—so the Dawn Fisher on your birth certificate can't be the same person."

"How do you know that?"

"Because I was there when she had her hysterectomy. Actually, that's not exactly—" Rebekah stops, takes a deep breath. "Dawn did get pregnant, when she was seventeen, but something went wrong with the pregnancy, and then she had to have the procedure. At that point, I was the only one in the family who was in touch with her."

All of this is coming at Madeline too fast. Too much. *Her mother had had a hysterectomy at seven-fucking-teen.* Almost fifty years ago. So she was clearly *not* the Dawn Fisher listed as Mother on Madeline's birth certificate, since she was born in 1984.

Rebekah turns to Sarah. "Do you want to...?"

Sarah says, "I treated your mother when she was a young girl. And, I might add, taking an Amish child to a psychiatrist was much less common back then."

Rebekah corroborates this with a nod, then they both look at Madeline expectantly.

"Treated her for what?"

Sarah glances apologetically at Rebekah, "I already told your aunt that I can't violate my patient's confidentiality." Then to Madeline, "However, I can say that, unless she's had professional help along the way, her issues will have impacted her behavior. And her relationships. Do you know if your mother has ever sought psychiatric help?"

Madeline feels faint. She grips Keira's leash, and Keira looks at her worriedly. "It's okay," she says touching the top of Keira's head.

Sarah and Rebekah exchange a glance, then Rebekah says, "I will say what Sarah cannot. Dawn—" she stops. "Kiki," she says firmly, "Kiki has a mental illness of some kind or other. I wouldn't know what to call it...but I told you she was different. Well, I think that's a cowardly way of saying that she was a *terror.* She stole. She cheated. She lied. Sometimes she was even...violent." She puts her hand on Madeline's arm, pressing it lightly. "But she could also be extremely entertaining and charming when she chose to be. I can tell she loves you very much."

Sarah says, "May I?" Rebekah nods.

"Madeline, you seem like a very loving and sensible person. Your aunt tells me that your mother is...acting out right now. When she comes back to herself, she'll need your help." She leans forward onto her cane and says, "I know it isn't easy to live with an unstable family member—"

"Hold up," Madeline says, putting her hand up for emphasis. She isn't sure how it happened, but this conversation is going off the rails. "Mom can be difficult, but she's not *mentally ill*. She's a successful business owner." She hears her own desperation.

All those clothes and things in the wrong sizes, the wrong colors, the wrong styles, thrown *violently* here, there and everywhere. *She stole. She cheated. She lied.* Her mother is a *terror*. And she's no closer to understanding the mystery of her multiple birth certificates than she was when she met these two crones.

They're both looking at her with that expectancy again, and that just makes her more angry.

"Well, this was a total waste of time. I don't know why I came here," she says. "Neither of you know my mother." She jiggles Keira's leash. "C'mon, Keira."

Distress creasing her brow, Rebekah holds out the bonnet, but Madeline says, "Keep it."

"I wish you wouldn't leave."

Sarah says, "Why are you so angry?"

And that clenches it. An echo of Kiki, so many times asking her *Why are you so angry all the time?* This old woman can go fuck herself.

She shakes off Rebekah's hand and doesn't even say goodbye, doesn't look back.

The scenery on the drive home now just seems depressing. Sad cows in the fields. Sadder dogs chained to their pathetic doghouses. Dead possums smeared across the road. The only bright spot is Keira who, blissfully unaware of human turmoil, enjoys the ride home as much as the ride there.

Raoul stands at the front of the clubhouse.

"For fuck's sake."

When he checks the fence behind Hole #18, he sees that not only have they cut through, *again*, they have literally removed at least a four-foot-square section of chain link. Quite neatly square. God only knew what they'd done with the missing piece.

"Motherfuckin' kids."

Raoul pulls out his phone, dials, waits. "I'm at the course."

"We're closed," Madeline says.

"Obviously," Raoul says. She sounds funny and he remembers that she'd gone to see her aunt, so he says, "I came by to clean out my desk, and I want to hear how your thing went, but first—"

Madeline interrupts, "Raoul, you're not quitting."

"Okay, but—look, somebody cut the fence again, and this time they trashed the clubhouse. The candy machine is toast. Don't even know if it can be repaired."

"What?"

"I'm looking at it right now. And it seems like somebody went at this place with a—"

"Baseball bat."

"No. I was going to say a golf club." Raoul spies a club still stuck in the sheet rock next to the men's bathroom. "Yup, golf club."

"Raoul, I'm sorry. I can't deal with this right now."

"Okay..."

"Can you please handle this? Call the insurance company, get that ball rolling?"

"How'd it go with your—aunt?"

"When you're finished making those calls, come by the house. We should talk. But I gotta go now."

Raoul stares at the chaos in front of him and the hours of clean-up it will entail. Only after that will he consider appropriate measures of revenge on the punks who did this.

Chapter 22

It's Your Birthday

Kiki wakes up with a start in her car, parked at a rest stop off 95 near Morrisville. Rain smears the windshield, but she wipes fog off the inside of the window with her sleeve to peer out at soggy grass and a single tractor trailer across the parking lot, smoke drifting from its tailpipe. Otherwise, she's alone.

She tries some neck rolls, the muscles so cricked she can't look to her left or right, the nerves zapping from behind her ear down to her lower back. She has to pee really bad, so she puts up the hood on her jacket and trots to the rest stop bathroom.

Two stalls but only three tissue-thin squares between them. She faces the mirror, flinching when she looks at the puffy pockets of flesh under her eyes and the terrible state of her hair. She takes a couple sips of tepid water, washes her hands, then her face, also with plain water (of course, there's no soap, what did she expect?) and smooths her hair as best she can. In her haste, she's left her purse (and her comb) in the car.

She really needs a shower and a change of clothes. And it's Madeline's birthday.

Time to go home.

She trots back through the rain to the car, noting that the tractor trailer has since departed. She combs her hair, sips from a plastic bottle of water she picked up when she stopped for gas the night before and checks her phone charge (forty-two percent). She slides it open and taps out a text.

Are you awake?

Nothing for so long that her phone times out, then *ping.*

Yes where are you?

Can I come by?

Now?

Yes

Again, nothing. Kiki holds her breath, then the message comes in: *Are you drunk?*

No

I'll make coffee

Madeline wakes up alone on her birthday. The note on the kitchen table reads, *Gone birthday shopping—see you tonight! xJ*

"What do you think of that?" she asks Keira Knightley. Keira immediately walks over to her empty food bowl and sits down, looking back over her shoulder at Madeline.

She and Jawari had stayed up till almost two in the morning, talking through her disastrous visit to Nockamixon and discussing alternatives for finding Kiki. Jawari is in favor of going to the police because Kiki is technically missing and possibly a danger to herself, but Madeline is reluctant to expose herself—and probably Raoul—to prying questions from the authorities that they don't have answers for.

Raoul. She'd almost forgotten. She goes back into the bedroom and unplugs her phone, then taps his number. It goes immediately to voicemail. *Where is he? Could he have gone looking for Kiki?* She opens her message app and types a text.

Thought we were gonna meet this morning. Where are you?

She waits. And waits.

Keira comes to the door of the bedroom and wags her tail, so Madeline gets up and takes her outside. When she comes back inside, a text notification: *Everything is fine. I'll catch…*

Impatiently, she slides it open. The full text reads: *Everything is fine. I'll catch you later. Happy Birthday!* And then a burst of party balloons float across her screen.

What wasn't Raoul telling her?

The day before Kiki wakes up in her car at the rest stop and decides to return to her other life, she parks in the lot of some church on 6th Street (*free parking*) and spends the daylight hours walking from one end of the city to the other, exploring parts of North Philly and then Center City (where she hasn't spent time in years). The nice weather has flooded the streets with tourists.

At Franklin Square, she watches the flow of mini golfers through the links, and it's as if she's a ghost come back to observe but not be part of corporeal experience. Parents with children trying to keep everybody on track. Couples in love holding hands, kissing, the golf beside the point. Groups of raucous teens competing for par on each hole.

She is invisible, her mind wiped clean, her former self inaccessible, and this present self only able to take her from moment to moment but not backward or beyond.

She heads back to South Philly and McGuyver's Tavern where she plans to begin the evening's festivities. On the way, on a deserted side street with narrow sidewalks and houses that come right down to the pavement, she sees a man sleeping on a grate, steam rising around him, his bare feet resting on metal, red and raw with cold. She looks away and hurries past. Then a bit farther on, at the cross street, she hails a city worker, gray-haired and harried, who's replacing trash can liners along the block.

"There's a man," she says. "I think he might need help."

The worker looks up, replaces the cover on the trash can, and takes in Kiki's disheveled appearance. "What now?"

"There's a man," Kiki repeats. "Down there. He's asleep on the sidewalk. He looks...cold. Maybe he's ill?"

The worker waves his hand. "That guy? He's always there," he says. "That's where he lives."

That's where he lives. The thought follows Kiki all the way to McGuyver's.

At the bar, she decides on bourbon and orders an old fashioned because it reminds her of Mr. Schmuck, even though they'd never been to this place (or at least she doesn't think so). The bartender is a hard-faced, muscle-bound dude with a shaved head and an unfriendly expression when he puts the drink in front of her.

"That's five bucks."

"I'll run a tab," Kiki says.

But Muscle Man shakes his head. "No tabs."

Kiki digs out six dollars, and Muscle Man takes it without comment.

An old man with missing teeth and a small, fluffy white dog takes the seat next to her, dog on his lap, while she idly stirs the drink. He orders a Miller Lite.

"Bottoms up," he says, holding up his glance and giving hers a clink.

She smiles but leaves the glass where it is.

"Aren't you gonna drink that?"

"I don't know."

He and his little dog are both peering at her with curious interest. "You're not a regular," he says.

Kiki stares at the amber liquid in her glass. She still has no desire to take that first sip. Her vision seems extra sharp, the glass, the ice, the maraschino cherry swimming in the bottom all in perfect focus.

He says, "Had a teacher name of Schmuck. Mrs. Irma Schmuck. Taught typing and health."

Kiki looks over at him. He smiles widely, revealing matching missing teeth on either side of his two front teeth. His little dog has a rather adorable underbite. He says, "Your jacket gave you away."

Kiki slides her glass toward him. "I haven't touched this. Would you like it?" Then, she chucks the little dog under its little chin, shoulders her purse, picks herself up off the barstool, walks out of McGuyver's and takes her first steps back home.

"I've made my decision," Leona says to Derek over a breakfast of pancakes and green salad (chemo gives Leona strange cravings sometimes) at an upscale (and overpriced) diner in West Chester.

"I'm just going to tell her. Today. On her birthday."

"Okay," Derek says.

"I believe she deserves to know," Leona says. "Whatever the consequences of that knowledge are, it has to be worth it. It just has to be."

Derek takes a thoughtful sip of his coffee. "Will you ask her to take a DNA test?"

"I don't need a DNA test." Leona's tone is sharp.

"Okay."

"I could ask. Doesn't mean she'd agree."

"No."

"Do you think I'm making a mistake not to involve the police and the FBI?"

Derek stops chewing in mid-bite, then continues chewing and swallows before he answers.

"That depends on what your goal is, I guess. If you want to punish Kiki, then we should definitely involve the police and the FBI."

"But?"

"But...if you do that you might alienate..." he still has difficulty thinking of that young woman as Janet "...your daughter."

"That might happen anyway."

"True."

Leona toys with the salad's unenthusiastic iceberg lettuce.

"You feel okay?"

She looks at him. "I'm scared."

Derek reaches across the table, takes her hand, gives it a squeeze. "How about some pie?"

"Can I take a shower?" Kiki asks as she comes through the door.

Wearing the yellow Chinese silk dressing gown she'd bought him (at least he thinks she bought it), Raoul says, "Hello to you, too" and waves her toward the bathroom.

"You look fabulous," she says, shrugging off her coat. If she's waiting for him to return the compliment, she doesn't skip a beat. "I won't be long."

From the kitchen, he shouts, "Have you had anything to eat?" He waits, then goes out into the hall. The bathroom door is closed, and he can hear the shower going.

She's in there for long enough that Raoul reads through his entire newsfeed and is now scrolling Neiman's men's sale pants, filtered for *black* and *size 34x32*.

When she comes in, she's back in her clothes (*appalling*), and in the bright northern light of his kitchen, the first word that pops into his mind to describe how she looks is *haggard*. He feels immediate guilt for hating how diminished she seems.

"Sit down," he says and gets up to toast some bread, throw an egg in the pan, be busy so he can prepare for whatever is coming.

He puts a mug of black coffee on the table. "I'm out of almond milk. You want sugar?"

"No, this is fine," Kiki says.

They're both tiptoeing through the minefield, and, if he's honest, this is kind of how it goes with her. There's always been something *tamped down*, something that signals *don't ask*. She had, on rare occasions, told him some things, alluded to a painful past, dark times before she adopted Madeline, her drinking problem and recovery, but what he's since found out makes him cautious about pushing her. What if he finds out something truly unforgivable?

He puts eggs and toast in front of her, pours them both more coffee and sits down across from her at the table.

"Talk to me," he says.

"I'm sorry. I really screwed up. But I'm better now."

"Well, you certainly *smell* better than you did when you came in. The other part I'm not so sure about."

"I *am* sorry, Raoul. I don't want you to quit. I'll fix this."

"I'm not talking about that." He says it more sharply than he meant to.

"Okay…"

"I'm not—look, we went into your place, when you disappeared. We were worried. Madeline was *really* worried."

Kiki pushes the egg around on her plate.

"You need to tell her the truth."

"Which is...?" Kiki says in a cold voice, still avoiding eye contact.

"How you got her. *Where* you got her. Obviously, you lied to me about her being *your* baby, about needing to *hide* her from her father. Was this an illegal adoption?"

Kiki shakes her head, stares down at the uneaten food.

"Who gave Madeline to you?"

Kiki bites her bottom lip.

"This doesn't look *right,* Kiki. It looks like child trafficking or something."

Kiki won't look at him.

"Please. I need you to be honest."

"It's not what you think. It's not any of that." She finally looks up. "I have a...a thing. A *condition.* Sometimes I can control it and when I can't..." She shakes her head, looks toward the window.

Rain patters. Raoul can hear his own breath. Kiki seems to be holding hers.

A condition. Was being a prolific shoplifter a condition?

"You *stole* all that *stuff.* I know you did it." Raoul's voice is a harsh rasp, and Kiki flushes. In embarrassment, he presumes. "Did you get Madeline *illegally?*"

Her head comes up. "I *rescued* her."

"Oh, my *god.*" Raoul's heart is racing. He shouldn't have had so much coffee. He's too old for this.

In a small voice, Kiki says, "Madeline is my good thing. My one good thing. You know that's true."

But Raoul thinks, *I don't know anything anymore.*

Chapter 23

Minefields and Mindfields

"Raoul isn't answering my texts," Madeline says first thing when she opens the door.

Jawari's smile fades slightly, and she tucks the bottle of champagne (*real French champagne*) under her arm and shifts the grocery bags to her other hand. "These are heavy. You gonna let me in?"

"Sorry!" Madeline reaches for the bags, but Jawari doesn't let her take them.

Dropping the bags in the kitchen, Jawari shoos Madeline away. "No peeking," she says. "There's more."

Then she goes out and comes back with a biggish, gift-wrapped box and a small bouquet of freesias (Madeline's favorite flower).

While Jawari fusses with arranging the flowers in a Ball jar she pulls from the cupboard, Madeline says, "I think my mother and Raoul are together somewhere."

Jawari looks at her over the top of her glasses. "Are you going to obsess over this all day?"

Madeline wrinkles her nose, looks away.

"We could go over to Raoul's place," Jawari says.

"And if he's not there...?"

"Then we have to wait for him to get in touch. If something had happened to either one of them, you'd know. The police—or the hospital—would contact you." Jawari pulls one gangly flower stem, trims the end with scissors and wiggles it into the middle of shorter ones. She pushes the jar of sweet-scented flowers toward Madeline, then leans forward and kisses her lightly. "Happy Birthday, babe."

Madeline says, "Do I get to open my present now?"

"Nope." Jawari turns Madeline around and pushes her gently out of the kitchen. "Now go take Keira for a walk, will you? I have stuff to do."

At the door, leash in hand, Keira waiting patiently, Madeline says, "After I get back, let's go over to Raoul's, okay?"

117

"Whatever you need. It's your day."

The steadier rain has turned to more of a drizzle, and Madeline is hopeful they might even see a bit of sun later. Keira plods along, sniffing energetically, shoving her nose down into the wet grass, squashing new green shoots with her enthusiasm.

Madeline had hoped to get to the course at some point and just make sure everything was still intact. Those kids were getting bolder, and, even though she dreaded it, she understood that eventually they'd have to involve the police—their insurance company would demand it anyway—but she hated the idea of it. Her experience with police is minimal but her personal encounters (especially that time she ran away for an entire twenty-four hours, and they found her sleeping in the cemetery), as well as her opinion of police behavior in general (*suspicious*), made her plenty wary of involving them. But these kids—well, they were *vandals*, weren't they? They had crossed a line.

Her mother had also crossed a line. Crossed many lines, probably. And now, Madeline wants the answers to all her unasked questions.

This is the longest stretch she can remember of not speaking to Kiki, at least on the phone. At college, she'd been the only one who talked to their mom every day. Perhaps more than most, she appreciates habit and welcomes routine, and Kiki has always loomed large in every aspect of her life.

It wasn't until she brought her first girlfriend home (at twenty-five) that she realized most other people her age didn't spend that much time with their mothers. Talia's mild observation that Kiki was possessive had initiated a big fight and, eventually, the break-up. *You're too close to your mom. It's not healthy.* That had rankled, perhaps mostly because Madeline had thought later, *maybe it's true.*

When Madeline turns onto her block, she sees Raoul's car parked at the house. She hurries Keira along.

Raoul is sitting with Jawari on the couch when she comes in. Keira whimpers when she sees Raoul and pulls on her leash, but Madeline grabs the old towel she uses for wet days and rubs Keira down before unleashing her to wiggle across the room, dancing on her front feet as Raoul rubs her ears, puts his face into her fur.

"Stinky girl," he says affectionately, then looking up at Madeline, adds, "Happy Birthday."

Madeline throws herself into the chair next to the couch, and Jawari gives her a bit of an eye roll. Madeline says to Raoul, "Where have *you* been?"

Raoul keeps his hand on Keira's curly back. "With your mother."

"Where is she?"

"She's home."

Madeline must have made a face because Raoul says, "Don't look like that. She's tired and wanted to be home. I told her she should take a nap."

"Where's her car?"

"Left it at my place."

"What the fuck is going on, Raoul?"

Jawari says, "Let's all stay calm."

Madeline says, "Bullshit" to Jawari, then to Raoul, "This is *bullshit*. She's *tired* and taking a *nap?* I want to talk to her." She gets up, and both Raoul and Jawari say at the same time, "Don't!"

Raoul says, "Please, Mads...sit down. I'll tell you what I know, but *you* need to know..." he stops, points between himself and Jawari, "...we're here for you."

Madeline sits down abruptly in the chair. Her heart is pounding in her ears. Keira wriggles out from under Raoul's hand and goes around the coffee table to press against Madeline's legs, putting her front paws on Madeline's feet as if she knows she needs to hold Madeline down, keep her anchored.

"Tell me," Madeline says.

Jawari reaches out and puts her hand over Madeline's gripping the chair arm and Raoul says, "Your mother needs help. Professional help. That's the first thing."

"I *know* all this already."

Raoul looks at Jawari who shakes her head slightly. He says, "Oh, yes, the shoplifting."

Jawari says, "It's officially called kleptomania, and it's usually part of a whole syndrome of behavior. I looked it up on Google last night."

"That's definitely part of it. But...there's something else," Raoul says. "It's about how you were adopted."

Madeline's stomach flips over and her heart flutters in her chest. "What about it?"

"She says she *rescued* you from a *bad situation.*"

Madeline looks at Jawari who shrugs and squeezes her hand. "What the fuck does that mean? What—who did I need rescuing from? My bio mom drowned. Or is that a lie too?"

Raoul nods. "That's the part that isn't clear. Yet."

Jawari adds, "Because we don't know how you got from the bad situation and needing to be rescued to being adopted by Kiki."

"But I think if we give her some time," Raoul says, "we *will* finally get the whole story, and after that, we'll just have to take it one step at a time."

Madeline says, "Why are you protecting her?" She looks at Jawari, then back at Raoul. "What about me?"

Raoul says, "Sweetie, it's all *about you.*"

Madeline gets up abruptly. "I don't want to know," she says.

They're all looking at her—Raoul, Jawari, Keira—all eyes on her.

"I don't want to know," she repeats.

Then she walks out on all of them, slamming the door behind her.

She was heading for the cemetery but turns toward the golf course because it has started raining hard again (she hates driving in any kind of bad weather), and it's closer. When she gets there, she takes a quick walk around the perimeter, just checking that the second temporary fence repair is still intact. It is.

In the clubhouse, she sees that Raoul has cleaned up most of the mess, but the soda machine is still pulled out and standing at an angle to the wall. The trashed vending machine has been carted away to landfill, the shattered glass swept up, and one broken chair has been shoved into the utility closet with the cleaning buckets, mops and brooms. The wall still shows a hole in the drywall where they'd smashed the club into it. The candy had to be tossed, but she finds a Snickers bar wedged under one of the small, round high-top tables where golfers gather to compare scores or take a snack break. It's still intact, so she opens it and eats it.

She should call Jawari—or at least send a text—but she's feeling stubborn as well as cross that Jawari didn't take her side more strongly.

Without thinking about it, before she can stop herself from doing it, she pulls out her phone and taps her mother.

Kiki answers on the first ring. "Happy Birthday, Mads," she says, sounding as if she's been working out, breathless, but otherwise just as she always does.

"Did I catch you at a bad time?" Madeline asks, and in an abstract, outside looking in kind of a way, marvels at her own ability to gloss over important moments with banality and politesse.

"Just cleaning up the house," Kiki says.

"Mom..."

"Are you okay?"

"Are *you?*"

"I'm better. Honey..."

"Why did you disappear like that?"

Long silence. But Madeline can hear Kiki breathing, so she knows she hasn't hung up.

Kiki says, "I'm sorry I did that. I should have—" she stops. "You're a lot stronger than I am."

"But you never ran away before. I'm the one that does that."

Kiki chuckles low in her throat. "Listen, it's your birthday. I want you to have a good day, so I'll do whatever you want. You want to talk, come over. You don't want to talk, that's fine too."

This is promising. Madeline says, "I'm at the course."

Kiki sounds confused, "Where's Raoul? His car's here." Madeline hears her mother rack the Venetian blinds. "Is that Jawari's car?"

Madeline winces. "We're back together. Well, I think we are."

"Is she there with you?"

"No, I...I got upset and walked out. They're probably still there. At my place. I should probably text."

"What were you upset about?" Kiki says.

"Why do you have fake birth certificates for me?"

Another extended silence.

"Mom...?"

"I needed documentation to get you into school so you could get a social security number." Kiki clears her throat.

"The names. They're all different. Who are they?" Madeline grips the phone next to her ear. "Are *you* Dawn Fisher?"

"Let me come over there. I'd rather do this face-to-face."

"Just answer me. Does Dawn Fisher even exist?"

"That was my name before I changed it. I put that name on the birth certificate—the one I decided to use—because it was my way of saying you were my daughter."

"So those other names are fake."

Silence.

"Is my birth mother really dead?" Madeline's voice is a whisper.

"I'm coming over."

And Kiki disconnects the call.

All the questions chase each other around inside Madeline's head. This time, she will get answers. She can feel it.

Chapter 24

Truth Comes at a Price

The silver-blue Camry is back, parked across the street and three doors down. The rain makes it hard for Kiki to see who's inside, but she knows the car by now anyway. This is going to be tricky.

She turns away from the window and surveys the bedroom, returned to order, everything back in its place, the mountain of clothes, accessories and shoes bagged and shoved into the back of the closet. She'll deal with that later, cut off all the tags, and drop it all at Goodwill. It isn't the first time she's turned that page, but maybe this time, she can stop. No, this time, she *will* stop. *Show humility, Dawn. Get right for her sake if not your own.*

Downstairs, she pulls on the rain jacket she's been wearing for days and goes to the kitchen door where she peers out toward Madeline's cottage. The blinds are closed, but there are lights on inside. Raoul's key fob lies on the kitchen counter next to her phone. She unplugs the phone and pockets the key fob, then opens the door, pulling it closed behind her, not bothering to lock—she needs to be quick if she's going to evade the silver-blue Camry.

She backs out of the driveway, making the turn as shallow as possible, and pulls slowly away, in the opposite direction from the Camry. She keeps the car in her rearview mirror, then turns the corner and accelerates.

She keeps an eye out the whole way to the course, but thankfully, no one follows her.

"Who's that woman?" Leona says. The man named Raoul comes out of Janet's house followed by a tall, dark-haired woman in chic glasses and a shiny pink raincoat.

"Don't know," Derek says.

"Well, who was in that other car then?"

Raoul and the woman seem to be arguing about something, standing there in the rain, then they both hurriedly get in the black Lexus and the car reverses out of the driveway and speeds off.

Leona says, "Let's follow them."

"Wow," Derek says, "I'm starting to feel like I'm in a movie."

"Well, then, step on it," Leona says.

Derek jams the accelerator to try to catch up to the Lexus that has already disappeared around the corner.

They pick up the car at the traffic light three blocks on. When it turns left, they do too. Derek is enjoying this, Leona can tell, and it would be kind of fun if it weren't also making her feel slightly sick to her stomach.

"They're going to the golf course," Leona says.

Raoul and Jawari are already getting out of the car when the silver-blue Camry glides into the spot next to them. The rain has finally let up, but the newly leafed trees create their own rain with every rustle of wind. Jawari's hair whips around her face. She looks at Raoul. "Who's that?"

"Not a clue," Raoul says.

They stand by the Lexus waiting as the couple in the other car gets out.

"We're closed," Raoul says with forced friendliness.

Derek says, "We're looking for Madeline Morel." He points at the blue VW parked next to the ticket booth. "That's her car, isn't it?"

Jawari says, "What do you want with Madeline?"

"It's a private matter," Leona says.

Kiki is surprised when she goes into the office and Madeline isn't there.

I'm here. Where are you?

Clubhouse.

Madeline is sitting on the low cement wall that abuts the clubhouse. Clouds scud across an ombre sky. Kiki sits down next to her. They watch the clouds for a moment.

"Remember that time Raoul got you tickets to see *Wait Until Dark* for your thirteenth?"

"*I cannot negotiate in an atmosphere of mistrust,*" Madeline says.

"You used that line for *years* to get away with all kinds of stuff."

"It's a good line. But I still think Tarantino was a sucky Roat."

This they could do. Talk trivialities. Talk around things, skating along the slippery surface to avoid plunging into rough water.

Madeline's phone vibrates. Jawari. *Call me.*

"Who's that?" Kiki asks.

"Hold on, Mom." She stands up and walks away, keeping her back to her mother. "What's up?" she says when Jawari answers.

"Are you okay? Where are you? We're at the golf course."

"I'm here," Madeline says. "Mom's here. We're in the clubhouse. Talking."

"Crap," Jawari says.

A woman's voice in the background says clearly, "Where is she?"

"Who's that talking?" Madeline says.

"There are some people here to see you."

"This isn't a good time. I need to talk to Mom right now."

"I know. It's just—" Jawari muffles her mouthpiece, and Madeline can hear only snatches.

…important!…another time?…wait!

The call disconnects. Madeline pulls the phone away from her ear. This is a real shitshow. Happy fucking birthday. She turns back to her mother. Kiki's on her feet looking toward *Hole #9.* Madeline follows her gaze.

The woman in the red wig is leading a parade, Mr. Bland marching protectively behind her, Raoul and Jawari trailing behind him. Jawari is looking at her like *what the fuck.*

The woman in the wig goes right up to Kiki and says, "Did you tell her?" Then she turns to Madeline and says loudly, "Janet, it's *me.*"

Raoul says, "Oh, *shit.*"

Jawari says, "Holy *fuck.*"

Leona pushes Kiki, who has stepped in front of Madeline, out of the way.

"I'm your *mother*, Janet," Leona says and jerking her chin at Kiki, "She's a *kidnapper.*"

Madeline looks at Kiki, then back at Leona.

Leona whispers, "It's *me.*"

Then, Madeline doubles over and vomits all over Leona's Nikes.

Leona calmly steps back, lifting first one foot, then the other, to escape the puddle of spew. She stares down at her shoes. "Oh, my," she says.

There is a moment of complete stillness; then everybody starts talking at once, and Madeline turns and flees into the women's restroom, slamming and locking the door.

Chapter 25

Everybody to Your Corners

"Well, I hope you're happy," Kiki says. Then she goes behind the counter and comes back with a roll of paper towels.

Derek takes the towel roll from Kiki as Leona limps to a nearby chair, succeeding in spreading the vomit across the floor.

Jawari skirts the mess and goes over to stand sentinel at the bathroom door. She knocks lightly. "Madeline? Can I come in, please?"

Raoul crosses to a door marked Utility and, using a key to unlock the closet, pulls out a mop and bucket. He rolls it over to the trail of spew between Kiki and Leona and starts to mop.

Kiki just stands there in the middle of all of it, somehow remarkably disengaged.

Leona hands Derek a soiled wad of paper towels, and they exchange a look (*we stepped into it now, didn't we?*) before he tosses the mess into the trash can, turning his head away as he does.

"I could have you locked up," Leona says.

Kiki looks at her blankly.

Everybody else freezes.

"You *belong* in prison," Leona says.

Derek comes over to stand behind Leona, puts a hand on her shoulder.

"You weren't going to tell her if I hadn't done it," Leona says. "She has a right to know."

"And as you can see, it's not exactly the birthday gift you were hoping it would be."

"What you did was so cruel," Leona says. "Don't you even see that?"

Kiki looks at Raoul, but he's head down, swabbing away with his mop.

Leona stands up, takes Derek's hand and says, "Madeline seems like a nice person. You obviously—" she stops "—you obviously *love* her, have *cared* for her. I know I'm supposed to feel lucky about that." She pauses. "But I'll never know what *my* Janet would be like now. You took that."

Leona lets go of Derek's hand, stands up and walks across the room to where Jawari stands guarding the restroom door. Jawari steps aside and, resting her ear against the door, Leona says, "Madeline, I'm sorry if I ruined your birthday."

Inside, Madeline stares at the door, its faux wood surface. Everything a facade. *You have always known it. Janet.* That woman's voice, soft, unfamiliar and familiar.

"That wasn't my intent. To ruin *your* life. I...I've been looking for you for a very long time. I never gave up hope you were somewhere...alive...and well. And you *were.* I just—"

The pause is so long that Madeline thinks, *Is that it? Are we done here?*

"I just wanted you to know that I'm sorry I left you alone that day. If I had been a better mother, I wouldn't have done that. I admit that. Can you hear me?"

Another long moment of anticipation, then Leona says, "I'm going now. I'll leave my number with your friend here. You don't have to call, but I hope you will. Whenever. Okay...well...Happy Birthday..."

Madeline hears the woman say, "Thank you, please take care of her" (presumably to Jawari), then other voices talking in low tones. It seems like everybody leaves because it gets dead quiet.

Madeline goes over to the door and quietly unlocks it, opening it a crack.

"You can come out," Jawari says. "Everybody's gone."

Madeline swings the door open. They look at each other, then Madeline says, "I'm okay."

"Do you want a hug?" Jawari opens her arms and Madeline steps into her embrace. When they pull apart, Madeline says again, "I'm okay."

"Do you believe her? Could she really be your mother?"

"I don't recognize her," Madeline says. "Her face, at all. But the voice...I don't remember *her*, but...I think maybe it's true."

"Pretty easy to find out for sure," Jawari says. "We sell those DNA kits right at the counter now."

"I don't feel anything."

Jawari takes Madeline's hand. "That's okay."

They look at each other.

"This is crazy town," Jawari says.

"Welcome to my world," Madeline says. She tugs Jawari's hand. "Let's go get Keira and get in bed and drink champagne." Then she adds, "At *your* place."

When Leona goes over to talk to Madeline through the bathroom door, Derek stands there, smiling awkwardly at the wall.

Raoul squeezes the mop one last time, then rolls the bucket out of the clubhouse to dump it.

Kiki says to Derek, "Would you like a soft drink?"

"Um," Derek says.

Kiki walks over to the soft drink vending machine, pulls bills from her jacket pocket and starts feeding them into it. She comes back with a 7-Up and a Diet Coke.

"Any preference?" Holding up the cans in each hand. When Derek still doesn't answer, Kiki shrugs, pops open the Diet Coke, takes a swig.

Derek says, "Can I have that?" He holds out his hand.

Raoul comes back inside, having left the rinsed mop and bucket to dry in what is now full sun, steam rising off paved paths and rain-slicked putting greens. The woman (*Madeline's* real *mother*) is standing outside the bathroom door, presumably trying to coax Madeline out. *Good luck with that one.* Kiki and the husband (he presumes) are just standing there, drinking soda. Raoul tries to catch Kiki's eye, but now it's her turn to ignore his signals, so he goes over there, even though there's a tiny part of him that would prefer to walk away and leave all this melodrama behind.

"Hello," he says to Derek.

"Hello," Derek says.

"What happens now?" He directs this question to Kiki.

She doesn't answer. He tries again, this time, looking at Derek. "Does my friend here need a lawyer?"

Leona calls to Derek, "Let's go!" She's already headed back to the parking lot, walking quickly, head down, and Derek scurries after her with a hurried *thank you.*

"You should call Bernie," Raoul says to Kiki. "He'll know what to do."

Kiki claps her hands to her face and bends over at the waist. At first, Raoul thinks, *Here comes the storm,* but then he realizes she's not crying. She's laughing.

"Oh, my *god*," he hisses. "*Stop* that." He takes her by the arm and half-drags her out of there because he doesn't want Jawari or Madeline to hear her cackling.

"You're making this worse," Raoul says, hustling her along.

"Mads threw up on *her shoes*! That's just too perfect."

"I don't know what you're on, but you're starting to scare me."

Kiki stops. "Let me go," she pulls her arm away, then in the next instant grips his hand with both of hers. "Don't be mad. I can't deal with all this crap without you."

"What about your—what about Madeline? Did you think about *her*?" He gently pulls his hand away. "Did you think about *me*? No. And you never do. I thought we told each other the truth, capital T. You just sat in my kitchen and *lied again*."

"But I couldn't tell you. I couldn't tell anyone. I thought I wouldn't ever have to."

"Oh, sweetie..." Raoul says. "I hope you're feeling strong enough to stay on the wagon, because I need a fucking drink."

Thirty-three years old. She should be *processing* what's happened, fitting the symmetry of that composite number into some kind of Möbius strip of life-changing events, but the factors refuse to come together.

"But...weren't you afraid of her? At first?" Jawari says, sitting up to refill their champagne flutes.

"I don't think so. I really can't remember anything...before or after until, like, middle school. It's just...blank. I feel like I was pissed off a lot. Growing up. And it's funny..."

"What is."

"*She* never got mad or yelled at me. Sometimes I wanted her to. I'd do stuff. You know, to try to get her to react, just to bug her. But she would never take the bait." Madeline's lip curls. "Leona, though. Just hearing her voice today..."

Jawari sits up. "What about her voice?"

"That's when I knew. It's not a specific memory, it's more a feeling, but I know she used to yell at me."

Jawari flops back onto the pillow, takes her hand. "Janet, huh."

"Don't call me that," Madeline says.

"You don't look like a Janet."

"Because I'm not."

"Okay..."

Stretched out between them, warming them both, Keira Knightley sighs, then gives a little dream whimper in her sleep. At the bottom of the bed, Cersei watches them, tail twitching, head resting on her paws.

"Don't you want to talk to this Leona person?"

"I don't know," Madeline says. "I don't think so. At least not now. I need to sort things out with Kiki first." She gets up, and Keira and Cersei lift their heads and watch her go out.

"Where are you going?"

"Need my phone. Left it in my jacket."

When she comes back, she holds up the phone. "Like, fifteen texts from Raoul." She climbs back onto Jawari's king-sized bed, and Jawari watches over her shoulder as she types a text back.

How is she?

Nothing at first, then bubbles, then, *Left an hour ago. In denial big time.* More bubbles and then, *She's going to need a lawyer.*

Madeline and Jawari exchange a look and Madeline types furiously: *And a psychiatrist!*

Bubbles, then nothing. Then the phone rings. Raoul says, "I don't think we should discuss this over text."

"Okay," Madeline says. "That's fine."

"How are you doing?"

"I'm *fine*. Some things make a lot more sense now. Look, I'm putting you on speaker."

"Hi, Jawari," Raoul says.

"Hey," Jawari says.

Keira lifts her head again.

"Keira's here, too," Madeline says.

"I made her tell me...how it happened, when she got you," Raoul says.

What had happened was that he'd told her he would walk out and never speak to her again if, this time, she didn't tell him the whole truth, capital T.

"She still insists she was rescuing you from a bad situation, but when I asked her how she knew that at the time, she didn't have an answer. Says she just *knew*. And, of course, how can we prove *that* after so long. Doesn't make it right, of course," he adds quickly. "This lady...your—" he stops.

"Her name is Leona Lerman," Jawari says helpfully.

Leona.

"Maybe we should go see her," Raoul says. "Her husband seems like a reasonable guy."

"I'm not doing that," Madeline says.

Silence. Then, Raoul says, "A lawyer could be helpful with the...psychiatric thing. I've been reading up on this stuff online. Kiki might be able to claim some kind of a fugue state or something."

Jawari rolls her eyes, mouths *I doubt that,* but Madeline waves her hand. "I don't want to be involved," she says.

Madeline's phone flashes another call coming in: *Mom.* She shows the screen to Jawari and Jawari's eyes go wide, pantomimes, *Answer it!* and Madeline mouths, *No.*

Madeline says, "She's calling in right now, Raoul."

"Talk to her, Mads."

Silence. A sigh.

"I will. Just not now."

Then Raoul says, "What do we do about the golf course?"

"Lock it up," Madeline says flatly. "We're closed for the foreseeable future."

When Leona gets back to the hotel, the first thing she does is throw away her Nikes. Then she lies down on the bed in her raincoat. Derek hangs his jacket up, then sits down next to her.

"Let me take your coat," he says.

"I'm good," Leona says.

"No, you're not."

"She really didn't know who the fuck I am, did she?" Leona says. "That bitch brainwashed her."

Anger makes her feel a little breathless. Or maybe it's the cancer. Either way, she feels like she can't breathe, so she turns onto her side, gasping. Derek gently pats her back, and finally she's able to get it (and herself) back under control, even though, for a moment there, her panic threatens to pull her under. Sometime soon, before her time (*so unfair*), her allotted number of breaths will run out.

Derek says, "Sometimes people forget things because it's easier that way. Self-protection."

"And I'm well aware of what traumatic memory loss is," Leona snaps, then immediately adds, "I'm sorry."

"It's okay."

She turns onto her back. "I'd love to see her in a prison uniform." She pictures Kiki, her neat silver bob shaved off, wearing an unflattering orange jumpsuit. "Did she look *old* to you?"

"Who, Kiki?"

"Yeah."

Derek shrugs.

"She aged. *A lot*. But I knew her right away." She takes her wig off and tosses it aside. "God, I'm so *tired*." She closes her eyes and seems to fall instantly to sleep.

Derek watches her for a moment, trying to imagine himself without her. It isn't possible. He gets up quietly, then reaching across, pulls the top cover over her. He goes over to retrieve his cellphone from his jacket and dials Blair Robinette. When she answers, he steps outside, keeping his voice low and the door ajar with the toe of his shoe. He starts by apologizing for calling on the weekend, then says, "I need a phone number for Raoul Berger."

"The guy from the golf course?"

"Yeah."

"How's it going there?"

"Touch and go."

"Is your wife okay?"

"I think so."

There's a pause, then Blair says, "Is it her? And the daughter?"

"Leona believes so."

"And you don't?"

"No, it's not that, it's...this young woman doesn't remember Leona, didn't recognize her. But I think Leona knows her own kid. I do think that."

"Oh," Blair says. "Well...that's tough." Then, more briskly, "I'll text you the number. Give me a few. Good luck with it, Derek. And tell Leona I said hang in there."

As his phone beeps the disconnection, Derek pulls his foot away and lets the motel door click shut after making sure he has his room key. He sets off toward town. He needs a beer. Or two.

Surrender is a strategy Kiki is well acquainted with. How you coped with it depended on what you surrendered to, and whether you retained even a small grip on solid ground. To be fully upright, feet planted, clean and sober, if a bit emptied out, on the brink of something *new*. Can she do it?

The sky is layered in pinks and violets, a perfect spring twilight. They'd be raking in the dough right now if the course were open, but when Raoul insisted they should close for a few days, she'd agreed. Besides, she'd much rather sit here and watch the sky fade.

If she has to wait to learn her fate, she will try to be patient.

"Dawn?"

Kiki twists around. "What are you doing here?"

Rebekah laughs. "You have terrible manners, Sister," she says.

"Have a seat," Kiki says, waving at the other Adirondack chair.

Rebekah peers at the seat in the half-light over the metal rims of her glasses.

"It's dry," Kiki assures her.

Rebekah perches on the edge, then gives a little surprised intake of breath when she slides into the reclining seat. "You might have to help me get back up," she says.

They sit for a few minutes in silence, watching the sky fade to palest purple.

"Getting dark," Kiki says. "Want to come inside?" She stands up, holds out her hand and hauls Rebekah to her feet.

"I can't stay long," Rebekah says, "but I wanted to speak with you about something."

Kiki slides a mug of coffee across the table. "Milk? I only have almond."

Rebekah shakes her head, takes a sip of coffee, and Kiki sits down at the table, the only sign of her inner agitation in her forefinger tapping the tabletop.

"So...?"

"Things have changed a lot since we were girls," Rebekah says. "Things are better for people like—people with problems. Our brothers and sisters have moved into this century, for the most part."

"Really," Kiki says, with a dry look.

"Look at me," Rebekah says, "Years ago, I wouldn't have been welcome into a relationship with the family at all."

"Aren't you lucky?"

Rebekah ignores Kiki's sarcasm. "And in terms of mental health," she says. "The way people—*families*—deal with it? Amos's daughter, Abigail, she's seventeen now...she struggles with anorexia. She sees a therapist and—"

"Spit it out, sister," Kiki says.

"I've been thinking about...things. Since the death of our father. We should have done more for you." Rebekah lifts her shoulders. "But *nobody knew what to do*. With you. For you. I want to believe things would be different now."

"So, what's done is done," Kiki says. "Isn't that what Mama used to say?"

"Yes, it is."

"Why did you come here tonight?"

Rebekah leans forward. "I didn't want to go without saying I *am* sorry... about those things I said to you, out of anger. That's not our way. It's not *my* way."

Kiki nods. She isn't about to apologize for anything she'd done or said, and she hoped Rebekah wasn't expecting that.

Rebekah adds, "And I'm sorry for your troubles."

Troubles. That almost makes her smile.

Her sister takes a breath, then gets up and pushes her chair under the table. "Thank you for the coffee."

"You took one sip."

Rebekah smiles. "I shouldn't even have had that little bit."

"Oh, right. The devil caffeine."

Rebekah lets out a belly laugh. "You always made me laugh, Dawn." Then she adds, "I'll pray for you and your daughter. I'd like to get to know her, but I don't think she likes me very much."

Kiki walks Rebekah to the door, and when her sister steps outside, Kiki says, "If we don't see each other again...." Rebekah turns and gazes steadily at her. "I know you didn't have to come here, and I—well, I appreciate it, that's all."

Chapter 26

Two Mothers

On Monday, Jawari gets up before Madeline is awake, leaving a note that she needs to get to the gym before work. Madeline usually feels a bit uncomfortable in Jawari's condo when she isn't there, but this morning, it feels...right. She takes Keira Knightley out for a pee, nodding hello to Mr. Myers, the old man whose condo shares a wall with Jawari's. He gives Madeline a denture-perfect smile, picks up his daily paper, says, "Cute pooch" and totters back inside.

Keira noses around—*new smells! Oh, boy!* Mr. Myers is right, she is a cute pooch. Madeline sits down on the low step, thankful that the golf course would normally be closed on a Monday, so she doesn't have to think about lost revenues. She does, however, have to worry about vandals breaking in.

On her way to Raoul's to drop off Keira, Madeline's phone dings with a text from Kiki.

Can we please talk?

Since she's driving, Madeline ignores it. Another ding.

I know you're angry that's ok u deserve explanations

Madeline flips on her turn signal and pulls onto the narrow shoulder. She stares at the phone.

I made a lot of mistakes u aren't one

Then: *of them*

Madeline hesitates, then taps: *In the car. I'll get back to you,* puts the phone face down on the passenger's seat, checks her side mirror and gets back on the road.

At Raoul's, Keira seems excited until she realizes Madeline is leaving her there; then her tail droops, and she slinks over to sit by the front door.

Madeline hands Raoul a cloth bag. "Here's her food and her pain medication."

Raoul looks into the bag. "Who's the banana for? Me?" He waggles it suggestively.

"Gross," Madeline says. "She gets a quarter of a pill shoved into some banana—the pills are already cut up—but make sure you give it to her before, not *with,* her breakfast."

"Mads, you wanna sit and talk? Have a cup of coffee? Or a cocktail?"

"I can't. I want to get to the office and put in a call to Adams Security. We need to get that in process, or the insurance is going to go up. This has gone on too long."

"So, basically, you're just fine?"

He turns away, shaking his head, and disappears into the kitchen. Madeline follows him.

"I told you I am. Don't you think I know how I feel?"

He turns slowly to look at her. "Do you?"

"Okay." She yanks a chair out and sits at the table. "Here's how I feel. Pissed off? Check. Confused? Check. But do I think I'm living some kind of tragedy right now? I don't, Raoul. Do I have a weird story?" She nods. "And so do lots and lots of other people." She spreads her hands out on the table. "I want to keep this in perspective. And I want you to know that I'm *not* falling apart."

Raoul regards her from across the room for a long moment, then says, "I'm proud of you, Mads."

Madeline takes a deep breath, gets up and wraps her arms around him, resting her head on his shoulder for a moment. "Love you," she says, and Raoul says, "Love you, too."

At the office, Madeline makes the call to the security firm and speaks with a soft-voiced young woman (*Amber*) who says the sales rep (*Steve*) is on another call but takes her number and promises her Steve will return her call very soon.

It's quiet and, for a moment, Madeline sits listening to it. Even though the walls of the trailer are paper-thin, she doesn't hear the birds or the traffic outside. Across from her desk, on the wall, is the photograph of the three of them in Austin, the time they celebrated Kiki's birthday there. They're standing with their backs to the camera, arms around each other's waists, looking up, behind them the Congress Avenue bridge over the Colorado River, and overhead, the sky is filled with thousands of swirling black dots that, only if you look closely enough, you realize are bats. Thousands of bats.

She remembers that moment, the sounds of their wings, their bodies leaping toward the night sky. It ranked as one of the all-time best vacations they'd ever had. Now, Madeline wonders what Kiki might have brought back from those private forays to the shops downtown while Madeline and Raoul swam and sunned at Barton Springs. She was always just *window-shopping.*

Madeline opens her laptop, types in her passcode, searches for "kleptomania" and is immediately drawn into a rabbit hole of psychological theorizing and *adjacent disorders*. Like, impulse control disorder and its sufferers' *failure to resist temptation*. Symptoms like *engaging in risky behaviors, lying* and *running away*. If Kiki had been a pyromaniac or compulsive gambler, maybe things would have turned out differently.

She still doesn't want to talk about any of this with Jawari who, after all, has shown a tendency to characterize the situation as if it were a Lifetime movie (*her family was normal and boring*), or even Raoul, who has apparently been anticipating some kind of a breakdown. But alone, she can look at things clearly, read about it in black-and-white, clinical language. *Put it into perspective.*

The door to the trailer opens, and Kiki comes in.

"Hi, honey." Kiki clasps her hands together, then shoves them into her pockets. She crosses to Raoul's desk (across from Madeline's) and sits down in his chair, swiveling to look at her.

"I can't believe you threw up on her shoes," Kiki says.

Before Madeline can respond to that, her phone rings. It's Steve from the security company, but she's having a hard time focusing on what he's saying, so she interrupts before he gets too far into his sales pitch. "Can we talk a little bit later, Steve? I'm sorry. I'm in the middle of a meeting." She thanks him and ends the call.

"What's your point?"

"I just thought it was ironic."

"That's a fucked-up thing to say."

Impasse.

"What am I supposed to call you?" Madeline says.

A pained look crosses Kiki's face, then she shrugs. "You don't seem to remember, but you called me Kiki for a long time before you ever called me Mom. Are you going to see her?"

"I don't know." But that's a lie. She's already arranged it.

"You must—hate me."

"I don't hate you."

"I wish I could explain."

"Go ahead."

"I can't."

Madeline stares at her mother, incredulous. Then she stands up, shoving her desk chair so violently it rolls back and, walking past Kiki without making eye contact, she says, "Well, when you're ready, give me a call. Until then, stay the fuck out of my life."

Madeline calls Steve from her car and sets a date for him to begin work replacing the current chain link with the security fence, installing the closed-circuit cameras and monitors and updating their computer software. *That'll fix those fuckers.*

Kiki's shouted promise to *get help from a professional* as Madeline walked out was pathetic. She'd given her the perfect opportunity to explain, and her mother simply couldn't (or wouldn't) justify what she'd done. Instead, she'd made jokes like they were co-conspirators.

Madeline's next thought comes unbidden: *Were they?*

Fifteen minutes later, she pulls into the parking lot of the Penn Greenery, a strip mall disguised as a town square, with traffic circles and yoga-panted people of every gender, drinking lattes everywhere you looked. She parks in front of Panera Bread and goes inside. She spots Leona's bright red wig and slides into the booth.

"You want something to eat?" Leona says. She has a cruller and a cup of what looks like green tea.

"I'm good," Madeline says.

"Thank you for getting in touch so soon. I'm surprised, I guess." She looks curiously at Madeline. "You're so different."

Madeline raises her eyebrows in response.

"You were such a passive little thing." Leona takes a bite of her cruller, chews thoughtfully. "I was a social worker for almost twenty years," she says. "Saw a lot of abused kids. Terrible things." She wipes her fingers on her paper napkin. "I'm grateful as fuck you were with *her* and not...hurt...or worse."

Madeline says, "Maybe I'll have that tea. Be right back." And she gets up and goes to the counter.

Leona watches her daughter while she orders her tea, *Madeline* smiling tightly at the counter clerk's cheery inquiries. *Her daughter,* a grown woman.

"Why did you go with her that day?" Leona asks after Madeline settles back in her seat with a to-go cup of tea. "What did she say to you?"

"I don't know. I don't remember any of it."

"And no memory of you and me before that?"

Madeline shakes her head. She feels a bit ashamed, but she isn't going to lie. They both sip their tea, and Leona pulls tiny bits off the cruller but leaves them all over the plate.

Finally, Madeline says, "What are you going to do? I won't testify against her."

"You won't have to," Leona says after a pause. "I decided I'm not going to pursue any legal action against Kiki."

"Oh," Madeline says. Then, "We appreciate that."

We. She and *her mother, Kiki.*

"However," Leona says. "You should know that she has a criminal record. For *other* things, of course, not kidnapping." She shakes her head wearily. "It's all in the past, I guess, but still. She has a history of...criminality."

"How do you know all this?"

"We hired a private investigator. We found you on Facebook. Should have done that years ago."

"Facebook didn't exist twenty-five years ago."

"True," Leona says. She smiles, and Madeline smiles back in spite of herself. "Do you have cancer?"

"Oh, the wig? Yeah. Lung. One good, one bad. *C'est la vie.*"

Madeline feels a stab of sorrow, looking at Leona's narrow, foxy face (not at all like her own), and then she says exactly what she's thinking: "Do I look like my father?"

Leona's head snaps back, and then she searches Madeline's face, and says, "Maybe. Around the lips and jaw. But he had blue eyes. You got the brown eyes from me."

"Were you married?"

"*He* was," Leona snorts. "And much older than me."

Madeline's not sure she wants to hear anymore, but Leona babbles for several minutes about her own mother (*distant, cold*) and her father (*always disapproving*), both of whom were also much older when she came along, and who died in a traffic accident when she was only nineteen. Her family story strikingly similar to the lies Kiki had told her and Raoul.

"We were on our own after my parents passed, you and me," Leona says. "I was such a *kid*. Derek could tell you what a flake I was. Well, you were there... but you honestly don't remember, huh?"

Madeline shakes her head.

"Probably for the best," Leona says. "I was a different person then too, you know?" Her smile is crooked.

After that, there isn't anything more to say, so Madeline says, "I should get going."

Before she leaves, Leona presses an envelope into her hand and says, "This isn't a card or anything sappy like that. Just if you ever find yourself in Niagara Falls..."

They don't embrace, shake hands or touch at all. When Madeline walks past the window next to the booth where they'd been sitting, Leona is still there. She's staring straight ahead and doesn't turn, so Madeline doesn't wave.

Chapter 27

Madeline and Mehitabel

Raoul agrees to meet her at the cemetery with Keira.

Her "mother" was actually a kidnapper.

If she is being forced to choose, *which one*? Back then, it wouldn't have been her decision anyway. It would have been Janet's.

Madeline leans her head back against the cool, smooth stone. *Mehitabel.*

Mads, 1998

"It washes out," Madeline says, holding the tube of Atomic Turquoise Manic Panic away from Kiki, then putting her hands behind her back.

"Give it to me," Kiki says, but Madeline backsteps. "You're not dying your hair with that stuff. You're too young."

"Three girls in my homeroom do it."

"Their mothers shouldn't allow that, but that's none of our business."

"I just want to try it on the front," Madeline says, lifting up a hank of her brown, side-parted, chin-length hair.

"But why?" Kiki reaches out a hand, but Madeline takes another step back, is almost against the wall. "Come on, honey. You have beautiful hair just the way it is."

"I hate it," Madeline says and throws the tube of Manic Panic at Kiki.

They stare at each other for a moment; then Kiki says in a small, hurt voice, "That's uncalled for."

"Fuck you!" Madeline says and, grabbing her jacket, flies out of the house, jumps on her BMX and rides away fast, not looking left or right when she peels out of the driveway into the street, legs pumping in time with a single thought: *She'll be sorry when I'm gone … sorry … sorry … sorry … sorry ….*

Raoul picked her up at the police station the next morning. The cops had come after some guy walking his dog reported her sleeping on Mehitabel Snyder's grave.

"Your mother's been a wreck," Raoul says in the car. "Up all night—well, we both were—driving around looking for you. I thought she was gonna pass out when the police called."

"I was *fine*," Madeline says. "*They* treated me like I did something wrong."

Raoul pulls his chin in. "Are you kidding me? You're *thirteen*, Mads. You can't just run away and stay out all night. *In a cemetery*."

"She must be mad at me."

"*I'm* mad at you," Raoul says. "Your mother is just worried that you're so unhappy."

"I'm *not*. But she treats me like I don't know what I want."

Raoul just laughs.

"Are you really mad at me?" Madeline asks, giving him the side-eye.

"Well, I will be if you go for Atomic Turquoise. With your complexion?" He wags his head. "You're an autumn, darling. Stick to the red tones. Maybe Vampire's Kiss?"

"Will you talk to her?"

"I will if you promise to pick a color that suits you."

When Madeline gets home, Kiki is in her bedroom (door closed), so Madeline knocks.

"Enter," Kiki says.

Madeline opens the door. Kiki is on her yoga mat, eyes closed, doing butt lifts. *Just as good for the core as sit-ups.*

For a minute, Madeline watches her mother, not sure how to broach an apology without sounding like *she* was in the wrong because she's not. "Sorry I threw that at you," she says.

Kiki curls her spine toward the floor, spreads her fingers out on the mat, takes a deep breath, then opens her eyes and looks at Madeline.

"Where were you?"

Madeline shrugs.

Kiki sits up, folds her legs into a lotus position and puts her hands, fingers curled upward, on her knees. A cleansing breath. "Are you going to do that again?"

"What?"

"Run away. Because I can't handle that."

Madeline hadn't run away again, in fact, had very much stayed put, but Mehitabel's grave still called to her when she needed to get away. The weeping willow carving, meticulous, graceful. The hand-carved inscription:

Mehitabel Snyder
1789-1814
Angel on earth & in heaven

She hears Keira's joyful bark before she sees her, and then Keira's all over her.

Raoul says, "I better not get a tick," and sits down in the grass next to her. They watch Keira nose around the nearby gravestones for a few minutes.

"She didn't eat all her breakfast," Raoul says. "But she did get the med."

Madeline frowns, whistles for Keira. "Do you see her?"

Raoul looks over Madeline's shoulder. "She's coming. Just slow."

They exchange a look over Keira's curly head when she ambles over to sit between them. "Did I do the right thing?" Madeline says.

"Which thing?"

"Keira."

"I doubt we can answer that question yet. She seems to be holding her own."

"I went to see Leona Lerman this morning," Madeline says. "After Mom stopped by."

"Oh. How was that?"

"You know...*really uncomfortable*. With *both* of them." Madeline makes a face. "But Leona says she won't press charges or anything like that."

They both think about that for a moment. Raoul says, "What else did you talk about?"

"I think she was disappointed I don't remember her. It's sad. She seems pretty ill."

"And I thought *I* had a dysfunctional family," Raoul says.

They look at each other and laugh, and Madeline says, "Now you have *two* fucked-up families."

They lapse into silence, then Madeline adds, "Who does something like that? I mean, it's one thing to steal a necklace or even a dress, but a kid?"

"Have you asked her?"

"She says she can't explain it. Like, it just...*happened*. So we're all supposed to say, *okay, you don't have to*? And that's another thing..."

"What."

"Leona asked me why I went with her. Why I took a stranger's hand."

"Oh," Raoul says, with a look of distaste. "She wasn't...*blaming you*. Was she?"

"Well, it's a legitimate question. And I don't have an answer either. I guess that makes me as bad as Mom."

Raoul says, "Give it some time. You're going to figure it out." He puts his arm around her shoulders. "You have me, and you have Jawari. The queers have your back." He stands up, brushes himself off. "Let's go play a round, what do you say? We have the place all to ourselves."

They wind up playing two. It's a gorgeous day, freshly washed sky and vivid color everywhere. They pretend they aren't losing money every minute they're closed—or at least they reassure each other that the closure is necessary to beef up what they can clearly see is lax security that endangers their profits anyway. They don't talk about Kiki or Leona or Jawari or anything except the game.

They're both good, but Madeline is a better strategist, and Raoul can be irreverent, so he sacrifices some accuracy in favor of goofiness.

"Did I ever tell you about the first time I played golf here?"

"You mean when you met Mom? Yeah. Like a million times." They're on the second round, *Hole #6—A Skunk's Tale* with the skunk-tail pinwheel obstruction, and Madeline is up by two, so she wants to keep her streak going. She lines up her shot.

"I heard from that guy Gary last week. Out of the blue. Weird coincidence, isn't it?"

"The beautiful guy who left you to walk back to Philly in your platforms? What did he have to say?" She takes the shot, and the ball glides neatly between the blades.

"Nice one," Raoul says. "He quit medicine. He sells real estate now."

Madeline laughs. "Wow..."

"I *know*." Raoul makes a face as he bends down to set his ball on the green, then straightens to line up his shot. "I thought maybe he finally wanted a date, but then he tells me he's married."

"To a...?"

"*Man*. Of course," Raoul says. "But nothing would surprise me."

At *Hole #9—T-Rexy*, they stop for a drink at the clubhouse.

"This place needs a facelift," Madeline says, looking around, trying not to think about the last time she was there. "We should start doing ice cream, selling branded putters or sweatshirts, something different."

She imagines the clubhouse with freshly painted white walls, tearing out the (*let's face it*) badly worn Formica counters and tabletops, and getting something more modern and cooler. No more vending machines and trips to the bank with buckets of quarters. Everything done with debit cards or digital pay systems.

"We'd have to talk to Kiki about it," Raoul says, which is true, so after that,

Madeline doesn't bring it up again.

Raoul wins by one and crows about it all the way back to the trailer where they've left their jackets.

The boy with the bat in his hand looks up when Madeline steps into the office. She takes in with one glance the broken glass covering the floor, the trashed papers, her purse turned upside down. And Keira, cowering on her bed, staring, terrified, at Madeline who holds up her hand. *Stay, Keira. Don't move.*

She puts out her arm to keep Raoul from coming in. "What are you doing?" she says, even though that's a stupid question.

He brandishes the bat. "Don't move or I'll—" he doesn't finish the sentence, but all Madeline can see is how close he is to Keira.

From behind, Raoul says, "This is ridiculous," and steps around her. He stops. "Keira!"

Madeline says, "Raoul, don't," and keeps her hand up—*stay!*—and thankfully, Keira stays put, visibly trembling.

But now they're blocking his exit from the trailer.

Raoul's already got his phone out, but Madeline says, "Wait a minute." The boy's eyes are wild with fear and adrenaline, and she doesn't want to provoke him.

"Just go," she says to him and steps aside, pulling Raoul with her.

For a moment, the boy stands there, then he lowers the bat.

"Please just *go*," she says.

With his free hand, he sweeps the papers off her desk. They flutter through the air, and he stomps on as many as he can on his way to the door, where he turns and says, "Nice watchdog."

Then he's gone—tearing off toward the front gate—and Madeline crunches her way across the trashed floor to Keira. Lifting her in her arms, she carries her outside.

Chapter 28

Gifts

"It was a total disaster zone," Madeline says to Jawari. "Glass everywhere. So we just left it like that."

They're sitting outside on the small, enclosed patio outside Jawari's French doors, Keira Knightley at Madeline's feet.

"I don't blame you. But you guys need to do something about this little gangster, or he's just gonna keep coming back."

"It's happening," Madeline sighs, then puts her hand down to stroke the top of Keira's head. "I remember thinking if he touches Keira, he's dead. And I was serious."

Jawari stands up. "I almost forgot!" She goes inside, then comes back with the wrapped birthday present and plunks it down on the small wrought iron table between their wine glasses. "When I went by your place after work, I brought this back too."

"Thanks for doing that, babe," Madeline says. "I'm just not ready to see her right now."

"No big." Jawari smiles. "Open it."

First Madeline picks up the package and shakes it a little and something inside moves, rustling paper. She pushes the ribbon off, then tears through the paper to find a plain black box with a lid. Keira is watching Madeline's every move with great interest—the sounds she's making could mean a treat.

Madeline lifts off the lid and pushes aside pale pink tissue paper. "Ohhh," she breathes and takes out the ten-inch-square oil painting of Keira Knightley, smiling, tongue lolling, in mid-leap, her curly coat and shining eyes captured with exquisite detail, behind her a blur of green. "Oh, babe," Madeline says, her eyes filling with tears. "I love it."

Jawari says, "Do you remember that photo? From that day we hiked up Round Top? The artist has a little storefront in South Philly. I think she really captures Keira."

Madeline nods, but she's finding it hard to speak around the lump in her throat.

Jawari leans toward her and says, "Move in with me. I'm ready."

He isn't Raoul's type. At all. Short. A little soft. And the mustache is curled and waxed, something he deems hipster-ish. Therefore: *way too young.*

"How old are you?" Raoul asks as soon as they order their first drink. (*Craft beer, of course.*)

Christopher (*not Chris*) says, "Old enough. How about you?"

Raoul feels himself blush, and Christopher leans forward. "I like men with a little gray."

Raoul sips his extra dry martini and watches Christopher while he tells him about his job (*freelance IT*), his family (*large and extended, Roman Catholic but tolerant*), his hobbies (*hiking, travel—Europe, the Far East—and theater, especially off-off Broadway because that's where the* really *interesting stuff gets produced*) and what he's looking for (*a long-term relationship, hopefully marriage, but god forbid, no kids*).

Raoul keeps his answers short (primarily because he hasn't done this in-person dating thing in a while and is still a little rusty with the small talk), but when he brings up that he works at Schmuck's Mini Golf, Christopher says, "I went to school with a guy named Schmuck. That must be a fun job."

"You play?" Raoul asks.

"Not regular golf," Christopher says, with a laugh, "but I love mini golf. I'm not very good," he adds.

Christopher orders them a second round, and Raoul starts to relax. This guy is easy to talk to in a way that surprises him, given their age gap, and when Christopher suggests they get together for a second date, Raoul finds himself saying yes, even though he isn't attracted at all.

When he gets back to his place, his phone dings and there's a message from Christopher: *Have tix for that Betty Davis solo perf next wk want to go w me?*

Raoul considers for a moment whether Christopher's auto-correct made it Betty with a Y or if he doesn't know how to spell Bette, but either way, he taps back: *Sounds good.* Then: *Thx for the drinks. It was nice to meet you* which elicits a 😎 *ill call you* in response.

Kiki keeps expecting to see Madeline's car pull into the driveway, but another day goes by, and the tiny house stays dark. She misses her daughter, a pain so keen she can't dwell on it, but she also misses Keira Knightley whom she thinks of as her dog daughter.

To stay occupied, she cleans and recleans her house from top to bottom, strips the twin beds in the guest room and remakes them up with fresh sheets (ready in the very unlikely event of overnight visitors), rakes the last of the winter leaves out of the garden bed, uncovering late season tulips whose leaves are yellow from lack of light.

She's on her knees with her hands in the dirt when Raoul's Audi pulls into the driveway. He gets out, tucking a brown paper bag-wrapped bottle under his arm.

"Looks good around here," he says and holds out a hand to help her to her feet.

She brushes dirt off her hands onto the thighs of her jeans. "What's that?" Kiki says.

He pulls a large bottle of Tasmanian Rain out of the bag. Kiki squints at the label, and Raoul says, "Nothing but the purest water from Australia, sweetie. Let's pour some over rocks and talk."

Raoul lays out the latest vandalism at the golf course and the plan that he and Madeline have come up with to tackle the security problems and renovate the clubhouse. "It's going to cost some money, but Madeline says we should be fine, especially since the upgrades, combined with a solid marketing plan, should bring in enough business to cover the outlay. We'll need to hire a couple of people, but probably part-time to start, see how it goes. What do you think?"

Kiki looks up, "About what?"

"Are you listening or...?"

Kiki waves her hand. "Whatever you two think we should do is fine. Madeline has access to all the accounts. You don't need me."

Raoul lowers his chin and looks at Kiki from under his eyebrows. "This won't be forever, you know."

"What won't be."

"She'll come around. Or maybe she won't. I don't know. But you can't give up. And I know you care about all this stuff, so don't pretend like you don't."

"How long till you reopen?"

"We don't have the carpenter's estimate yet, but I think *we're* looking at a mid-May Grand ReOpening."

Kiki pushes her chair back and gets up. She carries her glass to the sink and remains there, staring out the kitchen window at the tiny house, with curtains drawn against the bright April sunshine.

When she turns around, she says, "Don't you think I know there's something wrong with me?"

Raoul clears his throat nervously.

"I didn't know I was going to do that. I remember looking at her, sitting there covered in sick, and thinking *what a sad little girl you are*, thinking *I have to do something*, making that split-second decision. I know it probably doesn't make sense to *you* because a *normal* person wouldn't do that."

"Did Schmuck know?"

Kiki shakes her head. "I think he may have suspected something weird when I came back from vacation with a kid. He wasn't expecting that. I don't think he liked kids much, but eventually Madeline won him over. He used to let her count the cash and add up the deposits. He'd put that stupid green visor on her—I don't know how she even saw through it." Kiki shields her eyes with her hand to show how low the visor must have sat on little Madeline's head. "It made her feel important. He was a kind, sad man."

"Weren't you afraid you'd get caught?"

Kiki nods. "I think I've been scared to death for twenty-five years. Scared of somebody coming for me, scared of what Madeline would do if she found out." She sighs. "At least I don't have to worry about *that* anymore."

Raoul says, "Nobody denies that you were a good mother to her. Madeline understands that."

"How do you know?"

"She told me."

Kiki shrugs. "She wants to know *why* I did it, like there was some kind of premeditation on my part. That's the hardest part...to explain. I don't really understand it myself." She smiles crookedly. "If I did, I probably wouldn't have taken so many...risks. Or lifted all that *stuff*."

"What are you going to do with it?"

"I already took all of it to Women Against Abuse." She gives a little laugh. "They wanted to give me a donation receipt for my taxes. I declined."

Raoul says, "Derek Lerman called me."

Kiki stares at Raoul, expressionless.

"He's nice, you know. He wanted to tell me that they're heading back to Niagara Falls. He also asked if I could talk to Madeline about her—Leona. He seems to think it would help, you know, with the cancer and all, if Madeline were in touch." He stops. "It must be hard."

Kiki looks away.

"Have a little compassion," Raoul says. "The woman is dying." Then, his phone dings, and he gets up. "I should get going."

"Is that Madeline?"

"Christopher."

"Oh?" Kiki says. "And who is Christopher?"

"Just some guy I'm seeing."

"Some guy you *like*."

"Maybe."

"I hope *he's* nice."

"He is."

"Do you think I'm a bad person?" Kiki puts up her hand. "No, don't answer that."

She walks him to the door, and before he walks out, she grabs him in a hug. "I want to come back to work."

Raoul extricates himself gently and says, "We'll see."

Chapter 29

Bad News, Good News

On their return to Niagara, Leona takes to her bedroom (if not her bed) and spends hours in front of the television, moving from the bed to the chair and back again, never even settling on one program or movie, instead restlessly surfing and searching for something better, something that will sufficiently distract her from her thoughts.

It isn't as if she'd ever expected some big emo-fest of a reunion.

That isn't true. She *had* expected exactly that. This person (*Madeline*)—a cool customer (as Derek called her)—clearly saw her as the interloper and doubtless blamed her for destroying her relationship with Kiki. *Her mother.*

But was that relationship *really* destroyed? It seemed like the true nature of how Janet became Madeline hadn't even managed to put a dent in their bond.

As for her? She had felt nothing. And she felt nothing now. If she went there, it was a relentless voice telling her *you're dying what does it matter why did you bother what was the point what was the point what was* the point?

From the doorway, Derek says, "Lunch is ready."

Leona looks at him dully. "Not hungry."

Derek lets out an exasperated breath and walks out, shutting the door behind him with a slam.

Leona flicks the channel button listlessly, settles on some Vincent Price movie that would be funny if it wasn't so sexist, which actually is a bit of a distraction because it makes her a little angry. *As if movies today are any better,* she thinks bitterly.

Derek opens the door. He says, "Get up. We're going for a ride."

All of her protests and resistance are useless, so she takes off her pajamas and puts on a stocking hat, sweatpants and a sweater. They get in the car, and Derek takes 190 to the Rainbow Bridge checkpoint crossing where he produces their passports.

On the other side, Leona asks, "Where are we going?"

"You'll see," Derek says.

When they get to St. Catharines, Derek pulls into the parking lot of the

Stone Mill Inn.

"What are we doing?" Leona asks.

"We're having a romantic getaway," Derek says. "I packed clean undies and toothbrushes."

Leona looks out with a dubious expression at the imposing stone building. "I'm in sweatpants, Derek. I don't even have my...hair..."

"Nobody cares, and I plan to buy you whatever you want." He holds out his hand. "Come on, babe. Let's have some fun, what do you say?"

They check into a two-floor suite with a bathroom the size of their living room and a jetted tub, and while she gets into a bubble bath, Derek goes out to pick up some clothes for her. He stops in a boutique with eye-popping price tags and attractive, thin salespeople, picking out a long, flowing blue skirt with an elastic waist, a matching turban, and a cozy, marled tunic top with a high neck and low back in blue *space dye* (according to the young man with long hair tied into a man-bun who waits on him).

Back in their suite, Leona tries on the clothes, her reflection repeated endlessly in the mirrored bath.

"How do they fit?" Derek's voice on the other side of the door.

She swings the door open and turns around for him, then walks into his arms and hugs him tightly. "You did good," she whispers.

"I love you, honey," he says. Then, "Please don't give up, okay?"

They drive home the next morning after eating breakfast from room service, Leona remarking that it was a shocking amount of money to spend on eggs and toast, especially given the exchange rate, but Derek hushes her, and she has to admit the eggs really are good. If she's honest, this breakfast and their dinner at a French place the evening before (*vegan, who knew?*) are the first food she's eaten in weeks (*could that be?*) that actually tastes good to her.

This time they cross back at the Lewiston-Queenston Bridge which gets them to Dr. Sarris's office only five minutes late, but, unsurprisingly, they sit in the waiting room for twenty minutes before the nurse ushers them into the office. Dr. Sarris gets up from behind her desk and joins them at the sitting area with couch and chairs.

"How are you doing?" Dr. Sarris asks.

Leona and Derek exchange a look, then they laugh.

"Your trip to Pennsylvania was good then?" Dr. Sarris says, as if surprised.

"Oh," Leona says. "That." Another look passes between her and Derek. "I'm coping." And Derek nods.

Dr. Sarris looks from him back to Leona, then shakes her head slightly and opens the folder on her lap. "I've got your latest test results." She looks up and smiles. "There's a lot to be hopeful about."

Derek gropes blindly for Leona's hand.

"I won't call this a *remission*," Dr. Sarris says, "Yet. But there's been significant shrinkage in the tumor. When you finish this course of chemo, we're going to go into a holding pattern to see how you do before we discuss any further treatment options."

Derek is crying openly now and saying *thank you* over and over again until Dr. Sarris gets up and crosses to her desk, returning to hand him a box of tissues. He mops his face, and Dr. Sarris says, "Don't thank me yet. Just keep the faith."

Kiki watches Madeline get Keira Knightley out of the car and go inside the tiny house. For a few moments, she considers going over there, but Madeline will probably shut the door in her face, and she's not sure she can deal with that, so she stays put.

The house is clean, and there isn't anything left to polish, dust, or vacuum. She considers calling Raoul to see if she can get some information about how Madeline is doing but discards that idea almost immediately. He keeps Madeline's secrets just as he always has.

Because she feels a certain dark restlessness, Kiki fixes herself a faux cocktail with some of that fancy water Raoul brought her and pops a lemon wedge on the edge of the glass, carrying it from room to room as if seeking a place to land.

When she comes back into the kitchen on her second circuit through the downstairs, she stops at the window just in time to see Madeline emerge from her house carrying an armload of clothing on hangers. She opens the back door of her car and shoves the stuff inside. She doesn't look in Kiki's direction when she straightens up, just turns and goes back inside, coming out a couple of minutes later rolling her largest travel Rollie bag. She stows that bag in the trunk of the car. Then she goes inside once more.

She's moving out.

After another moment, Madeline comes back outside, locks the door behind her, gets in the car and drives away without a single glance toward the big house, toward Kiki standing in the window willing her to *look over here*.

She didn't take Keira. So maybe Kiki has one last chance to get Madeline alone, say the right words, to make her see what it was like when she first laid eyes on little Janet sitting at that table, abandoned by her mother and covered in vomit.

Kiki had never hesitated, never entertained second thoughts once she took that little girl's hand. She had simply moved from one moment to the next, improvising her newfound motherhood as she went along, knowing deep down that she was saving herself as much as she was saving Janet.

It was Mr. Schmuck who had helped her with the birth certificates when it came time to get Madeline into school. She'd only asked him because she was desperate and couldn't think of anybody else to ask. When he naturally was curious about why she needed this documentation, she implied that it was too dangerous to tell him why Madeline didn't have a birth certificate in the first place. So he nodded and told her he'd see what he could do, that he knew *some people* who might be able to help. And he had come through. He had to have known something was *off,* but he never said a word to indicate suspicion or doubt about Kiki's story. Not ever.

What would he have said about it all, if he were still alive? She couldn't imagine he'd have stuck by her, knowing the truth.

That she was a *kidnapper.*

She didn't like labeling herself that way, but everybody who knew what she'd done thought of her as exactly that.

And a common thief.

Her father Ezra's voice in her head.

She wishes her sister had never shown up, because now she hears that voice all the time, and it really makes her want to

Drink.

Kiki puts her glass down on the counter, then grabs the spare key to Madeline's place.

She expects to hear Keira Knightley bark a greeting when she fits the key into the lock, but even when she opens the door, she hears nothing other than the ticking of the gas heat.

"Keira!" she calls. She can see from the doorway that the dog is not in the main room. She must be in the bedroom. Kiki slips off her loafers and pads across the pale wood floor. "Keeeiiirraa," she croons.

When she opens the door to Madeline's bedroom, it takes her a couple of seconds to understand what she's seeing: Keira on her side in the middle of the carpet, legs stretched rigidly in front of her, panting heavily, eyes rolling. She whimpers.

Then Kiki springs into action, pulling the blanket off of Madeline's bed and wrapping it around the trembling, whimpering dog, using it like a sling to hoist that forty pounds of dead weight and carry Keira to the car.

Kiki phones the vet on her way, trying to focus equally on making sure Keira's still breathing, laid out on her blanket in the back seat, and keeping the car on the road. She prays she doesn't get stopped for speeding and, at one intersection, blows right through a stop sign, receiving a blaring horn and an angry middle finger from a man in the Volvo.

At the vet, she leaves the car running and the door yawning and rushes into the waiting room where a calm-voiced vet assistant guides her to an exam room. Agonizing seconds pass while the vet assistant pages Dr. O'Sullivan, and Kiki keeps her hand on Keira's head, murmuring *it's okay it's okay it's okay.*

They take Keira away, telling Kiki in soothing tones that they'll be back as soon as they can to let her know what's going on, but Kiki can see O'Sullivan is concerned, his usual smiley expression turned sorrowful and clipped. After they go, Kiki can't sit still, so she goes out to the front desk and tells them she'll wait in her car and leaves her number.

Once inside the safety of the car, Kiki breaks and lets herself cry for a few minutes. Then with shaking fingers, she dials Madeline. *Please pick up.*

"Mom?" Madeline says cautiously because Kiki opens her mouth, but nothing comes out at first. "Are you there?"

"I'm here," Kiki says. "At the vet. It's Keira." Then she starts to cry again, and the line goes dead.

"She's okay, but we're going to keep her overnight," Dr. O'Sullivan tells them, all three standing around in the empty examination room. "She's had a seizure, and we want to do some tests to see if we can figure out what's going on."

"Can we see her?"

"Sure," he says, and leads them into the kennel room, which sets off a chorus of barking from the canine patients. Distantly, some cat yowls.

Keira is lying on her side inside one of the kennels and only wags her tail weakly when she sees Madeline and Kiki.

"Can I open the door?" Madeline asks.

Dr. O'Sullivan comes around and unlatches the door. "Try not to get her excited. She's hooked up to an IV."

They take turns giving Keira a gentle pat; then Dr. O'Sullivan clears his throat, and Madeline reluctantly steps away.

"You're my best girl," Madeline says softly to Keira before she turns to Dr. O'Sullivan, "How long till you have the test results?"

Outside, with Dr. O'Sullivan's reassurances reassuring neither of them,

Madeline nevertheless says, "I should thank you."

"I'm sorry I went in your place without permission."

Madeline rolls her eyes and walks away, toward her car. Kiki follows her. "I saw you moving out," she says. "Were you even going to say goodbye? I thought maybe I wasn't going to see either one of you ever again."

"You're so *dramatic*," Madeline says.

"Well, *are* you?"

"Am I *what*?"

"Moving *out*."

"Yes." Madeline turns around, her car keys in her hand. She glances at a woman holding a cat carrier who seems overly interested in their conversation, and says, "Mind your own business."

The woman scurries toward the door, and the cat lets out a piercing howl. Madeline says, "Let's go somewhere else if you want to talk, okay?"

It seems significant to Kiki that Madeline chooses the IHOP on Route 30, but it *is* the closest place where they might find a quiet table to talk.

Inside, the restaurant is deserted, and the girl at the podium hands them menus and tells them to *take their pick* so they choose a booth in the back.

"What can I get you ladies?" Their server is a round young man with a scraggly beard, an enthusiastic manner and a name tag that says BENN.

Neither of them has looked at the menu yet, but Kiki says immediately, "I'll have the Rooty Tooty Fresh and Fruity," which produces a sour look from Madeline. "C'mon, honey," Kiki says. "For old times' sake?"

Madeline slams her menu shut and says, "Okay, make it two. And I'll have a coffee."

"None for me, thanks," Kiki says and when Benn leaves, she folds her hands together on top of the table and says, "So..."

"So..."

"You're moving in with Jawari?"

"She asked me to."

"And you want to do it?"

"Obviously."

Kiki toys with her fork until Benn arrives with their pancakes and Madeline's coffee. "Enjoy!" he says loudly. After he walks away, Kiki says, "They don't give you as much whipped cream as they used to."

They eat for a while in silence, then Madeline puts her fork down on the plate. "I shouldn't have left Keira behind. She's been a little wonky for the last couple of days, so I thought it would be better if she stayed put while I dealt with everything." She looks at Kiki. "I feel terrible I wasn't there, and you had to deal with it."

"I love Keira," Kiki says. "You know I do."

"I know..."

"I hope..." Kiki hesitates. "I hope she's going to be okay."

"Me too."

"I'm glad I was there."

"Me too." Madeline turns her head to look out the window.

"I know you think I'm a horrible person," Kiki says.

"You're not—"

"Well, it was a horrible thing to do to you. And that woman—your mother—she didn't deserve...*that*."

Madeline still stares determinedly out the window.

"I want to make amends, be a better...person. But I can't change the past. And I don't know that I would, even if I could."

Madeline swivels her head and stares at Kiki with an unreadable expression. "Do you promise not to take this the wrong way?"

"What."

"Promise."

"Okay. I promise."

"Do you mean it?"

"Yes. What."

"I've already told Raoul that I won't be coming back to work when we— when *you* reopen the golf course in May."

Kiki looks stricken.

"I need a change. A big change."

"I see," Kiki says.

"It's time for both of us to change, Mom," she says. "We can't do that together anymore."

Madeline puts her hand out on the table, palm up.

Kiki stares at the hand—an invitation, an ending, a beginning—and then, Madeline wiggles her fingers. Kiki places her hand on top of Madeline's. Their fingers twine.

Chapter 30

ReOpening

Waking up with Christopher feels remarkably *normal,* now that they've "been together" for just shy of three months. Raoul measures coffee into his Melitta cone (five *flat* scoops for his; three additional *rounded* scoops for Christopher's), then fills the electric kettle with water and flicks the on switch. While the water heats up, he grabs his phone off the counter and opens the back door. May smells delicious. And while it's definitely partly cloudy, the breeze has no bite, so the weather appears to be cooperating with the Grand ReOpening of Schmuck's Mini Golf.

Come Visit Our Freshly Refurbished Clubhouse!
Try All Six Flavors of Our Homemade Frozen Custard!
Tournaments Trophies and More!
Rounds 50% Off for Adults
Children under 12 Play for Free

It's been a long haul to get here, but he's looking forward to today. He steps out the back door and dials Kiki. She answers on the first ring.

"I'm up," she says.

"That's not why I called."

"Okay, why'd you call?"

"I've been talking about things with Christopher," he says, "and I want to get this out in the open."

"Oh?"

"He's helping me recognize some of my *triggers.*"

"Ah-ha."

Raoul sits down on the back step. "You're not making this easier, you know."

"What do you want me to say? You're talking about me to your boyfriend."

"I'm not talking about *you.* I'm talking about *me.*"

Silence.

Raoul says, "Kiki, you've been my best friend for a long time. Christopher is not a replacement. He's an *addition*. Can't you be happy for me?"

"I never see you anymore."

"We *work* together, eight hours a day, every day except Monday."

Silence.

"I know all the change is hard for you."

Silence.

"You really need to see someone."

"I'm going to," Kiki says finally. "I already made an appointment."

Christopher opens the back door and Raoul half turns and puts his finger to his lips. Christopher mouths *Is it Kiki?* and Raoul nods. Christopher discreetly backs away and closes the door quietly.

When Raoul comes back inside, Christopher has poured both their coffees and is sitting at the table, scrolling news on his phone. Without looking up, he says, "And how's Kiki?"

"Not sure." Raoul picks up his coffee and takes a sip.

Christopher says, "Do you mind if I get there a little late today? I have to go get somebody a Grand ReOpening gift."

Raoul comes over and puts his arms around Christopher, plants a kiss on top of his tousled head, says, "Mmm, you smell like wood smoke."

Christopher laughs and tilts his head back. They kiss.

"I knew you'd be here early," Madeline says when she finds Kiki in the office at her desk in front of her new computer at 8:45.

Kiki squints at the screen, then sits back with an exasperated sigh. "My password's not working."

"Ugh..." Madeline goes over and leans over Kiki's shoulder.

"I thought it was knightley57," Kiki says, "but it's not working."

"I told you to put all your passwords into one spreadsheet or at least write them down in one place. Try Knightley with a capital K."

Kiki taps in the corrected password, and the computer desktop appears. She smiles up at Madeline. "My brilliant daughter," she says.

Madeline winces and steps away, turning to go over to her old desk. She sits on the edge.

"Where is Keira, anyway?" Kiki turns back to the computer.

"Jawari's bringing her this afternoon. She's still adjusting to the chemo. Dr. O'Sullivan says we might have months or even a year or two at this point."

"I'm glad you decided to do that. I thought you should have done that in the first—" Kiki stops. "Well, it's all water under the bridge now."

Madeline makes a face at her mother's back, then says, "How's the new bookkeeper working out?"

Kiki shrugs. "Kind of serious. He and Raoul are thick as—" she stops, finishes with, "Gay solidarity, I guess. Raoul thinks I'm *jealous* of Christopher. Isn't that *ridiculous*?"

"It's hard when your friends hook up and you're alone. I've been there."

"Pfft," Kiki shrugs, then looks over her shoulder at Madeline. "You *are* brilliant, you know."

"Stop it."

She turns back to her computer. "Well, I appreciate you coming today. It means a lot."

"Wouldn't miss it."

"Oh!" Kiki says. "Look at that. Fourteen new likes on our page."

"Listen," Madeline says, "I have something to tell you."

Kiki holds up a finger. "Hold on, I'm almost finished this post. I uploaded this great picture of Rexy with the new clubhouse in the background." She hits *Post*, then swivels her chair to face Madeline. "What."

"I'm changing my name."

"What?" Kiki blinks incomprehension. "Why?"

Madeline stands up, puts her hands in her pockets. "I just need to, that's all. I don't want to be...Madeline Morel."

"Okay..."

"It's not anything about you...or us...or even *her*. You need to know that this is something I really need right now. I've called Bernie and he says he can help me. It's a pretty easy process. Well, except for changing my social security card and my credit and banking."

"That's a lot of changing. I should know."

For a moment, neither of them says anything.

"So, what's your new name?"

"Mehitabel Lerman."

"That's a...mouthful."

"I talked it over with Derek and he approved. He thought Leona would have liked that."

Kiki swivels back to her computer.

"Hey, are you okay? Mom?"

Kiki just waves a hand, and when minutes go by with the only sound the clacking of computer keys, Madeline says finally, "I'll go see if I can help Raoul."

After all the ribbons have been cut, and the Grand ReOpening crowd—filled with six different flavors of frozen custard and half-price golf and jokey tournament trophies—and friends and family and Keira Knightley have been sent on their way, Kiki is the only one left in the office. They'd had a mini celebration with the new staff (Bookkeeper Boy and Ticket Girl, as she thinks of the new employees) with champagne (for everyone else) and a large sheet cake with a well-rendered T-Rexy piped onto the top with ~~Schmuck's Mini Golf Grand ReOpening~~ in script around it, and she showed her best happy face even when Christopher cornered her and asked her *personal questions* that she evaded as politely as possible while sipping on her Coke.

He has a lot of nerve. They really don't know each other that well. But of course, he *thinks* he knows her because of Raoul, but that doesn't make it so. It's galling.

She is dreading the therapy session scheduled for Monday, but she is committed to going if for no other reason than to prove that she isn't afraid. Even though she is afraid. Even though she doesn't want to—doesn't know if she even can—tell it like it is, tell it like *she* is. There are certain things that neither Madeline nor Raoul would ever understand. She has never understood them herself.

What did they say about the unexamined life, that it wasn't worth living? For her, it was the only way she knew to survive.

It's still light out when she sets the cameras to *record*, logs out, locks the trailer and the big, new security gate and gets in her car. Tomorrow would be another busy day, then they'd have Monday off and then time would tell if this big investment in renovation and renewal was going to pay off. If today was an indicator, it certainly seemed like they could wind up having their best season yet.

When she pulls up to turn onto the street, she has to wait for three lanky teenage boys in jeans and hoodies, rolling toward her on skateboards, a parade of effortless athleticism in their swaying hips and perfect balance. As the third boy passes in front of her car, he turns and looks directly at her from under his hoodie.

She registers the face just as the boy lifts his arm and, with deliberate malice in his eyes, raises his middle finger at her.

Then he's gone, racing along the street to the corner and making the turn in perfect synchronization with his friends.

Kiki sighs. When she turns onto the street, instead of going right toward home, she turns left and heads toward I-295.

In Center City, she parks at the Convention Center and crosses to the Reading Terminal Market. It's packed with people. And hot. She has to take her jacket off almost immediately. But she's in no hurry. She strolls along, just looking.

At a fruit stand, she picks up a beautiful green apple from a pile of flawless fruit. The young women behind the counter are waiting on other customers. When the red-haired, freckly one hands her customer their change, she smiles at Kiki. "Just the apple?"

"Yes, please."

After Kiki pays, she takes a big bite of the apple and the clerk says, "They're delicious, aren't they?"

Kiki nods, smiles and moves on. She buys a large bunch of thin, pale asparagus (*local*) and six sticky buns from Beiler's.

When she comes out of the market, she realizes how noisy it was because even with the traffic and the crowded sidewalks, it's much quieter outside than it was inside. She sets off uptown, swinging her bag, taking her time.

She gets back to the parking garage only after it's fully dark and her parking has reached the $36 max. In the car, she eats two of the sticky buns, wiping her fingers on a crumpled tissue shoved into the passenger's seat cushion. When she tosses her jacket onto the back seat, a prettily flowered, delicate scarf falls out of the sleeve.

Kiki turns the key and, backing out of the parking space, rolls toward the exit sign.

Chapter 31

One Year On

"How's my girl?" Raoul says, coming into the office and plunking himself down at his desk.

"You talking to me?" Sam looks up from his computer (which used to be Madeline's), and Raoul laughs.

Keira Knightley's tail thumps, watching Raoul from her bed next to Sam, her head resting on her front paws.

"Did you see that reservation for Wexler Industries Executive Day?" Sam says.

"Got it," Raoul says, then frowns at his phone.

Just landed Athens GORGEOUS

"What," Sam says.

Raoul looks up, "Kiki's in Greece. Just landed."

"I'm jealous," Sam says, pushing his chair back.

"Honey, you and me both," Raoul puts his phone face down on his desk. "Christopher and I *might* take a run to Ocean City for a long weekend in July, but only the big boss gets to go on vacation in the busy season."

"Well, it's *off*-season in Greece anyway," Sam says. "She's gonna fry with that fair skin." He chuckles.

Later, Sam goes to lunch and Raoul is alone, so he texts Madeline (silently correcting the name to *Mehitabel*, resolving to edit her contact yet again if he can figure out how).

K safe landing in Greece just heard

He doesn't get a response right away, so he figures she and Jawari must be busy doing honeymoon kinds of things.

"It's just you and me, girl," he says to Keira, and she gets up then, stretching herself and shaking off before trotting over to him, looking at him expectantly. "I didn't say anything about a cookie." Keira's tail wags the second he says the word *cookie,* so Raoul reaches into his desk to get the treat bag and doles out one, then another, flipping them into the air for Keira to catch. Then he rubs her curly head. "Good girl, such a talent."

His phone buzzes.

I heard She just texted me 😊 *how's it going there?*

Raoul stares at his phone. It's going fine. At least he thinks so.

All good here. Tell J i say hi Have fun 🩶

He's glad Kiki is finally coming out of what he would characterize as The Bleak Times after Madeline (*Mehitabel*) quit and moved in with Jawari. He worried for a long time whether the therapy was helping Kiki *at all.* She seemed distant, shut down, inaccessible and chilly. But then she surprised him by inviting them—*you and Christopher, of course*—to her place for dinner one rainy March night.

They'd had a blast. Christopher brought Jenga, and they laughed their asses off over that one because Kiki beat them both three times in a row even though it was the first time she'd ever played.

The following week, he'd come in one morning to find that Kiki had taken all the photos of Madeline and her and him off the walls, even the one of her and little Madeline with old Arthur Schmuck himself in front of Rexy when she was brand-new. She'd replaced the photos with chrome-framed vintage movie posters. *Imitation of Life. Now, Voyager. Stella Dallas. Mildred Pierce.*

It hadn't escaped Raoul's notice that all these movies featured screwed up relationships between mother and daughter, but he'd never asked her about the switch in office décor, even though he missed seeing the photos of Madeline (*Mehitabel, for god's sake*) through the years and privately thought golf-related movie posters might have been more...relevant.

But, after that, things just got *easier* with Kiki in general, and he realized he'd been holding his breath around her. Now he could finally relax. That made Christopher happier.

The Greek trip had been a surprise. She said she'd seen some special on TV about antiquities and myths and then, because it was the hot season, she'd gotten her airline tickets for a *steal* (irony intended). And off she'd gone without a backward glance.

Raoul hooks Keira's leash to her collar, and they go outside. It's a hot day, and the course is busy. He waves to Barry and Darrell who now come on Fridays to play because it's buy-one-get-two-punches-on-your-Frequent-Golfer-card day, then walks Keira toward the street.

His phone dings.

It's a photo.

Kiki. Standing between two ancient-looking columns, the light bright behind her, face in shadow, arms stretched so that her fingertips touch each column.

And the words: *wish you were here! x*

The Sterling is everything Jawari promised when she proposed spending their honeymoon in Niagara Falls. The linens are crisp, and the jetted tub is big enough for four people, let alone two. They spend the entire first day in their room—with room service for every meal—and Jawari doesn't bring up the fact that Kiki missed the simple ceremony in the judge's chambers because she was already on her way to the airport to catch her flight to Greece. Raoul had come, of course, with Christopher. Jawari's parents had sent them beautiful corsages which surprised them both. Her coworker, Annie, had stood in for a second witness with Raoul. And Keira Knightley had been there too, of course. Everybody cried, and then they'd all gone out to an early supper celebration at a Greek restaurant where Christopher had booked them a private dining room (his wedding gift).

Jawari comes out of the bathroom, wearing the fluffy robe provided by the inn and showing a lot of very nice leg. She jumps onto the bed. "I *love* this place."

Mehitabel laughs. "You look fetching in that robe."

"Do I? What are you going to do about it?"

After that, they lie around for a while, cuddling and watching some old movie on the big-screen TV. By the end, they've both decided the movie is sexist *and* unrealistic.

They're getting ready to go out for dinner at a restaurant they pick from the list provided by the inn when Mehitabel's phone dings a message. She picks up the phone and looks at Jawari. "It's Derek."

I'd love to see you. When/where do you want to meet?

"He wants to know when and where we should meet."

Jawari looks up from adjusting her new earrings, freshwater pearl drops, a wedding present from Mehitabel.

"How about the falls? We were going to go anyway."

So Mehitabel types: *We were hoping to visit the falls tomorrow—meet there? Noon?*

For a minute, she isn't sure she's going to hear back, then: *That sounds good. Let's meet at the Hurricane Deck.*

Derek is nervous. It's now ten minutes past noon, and he wonders if he somehow missed her.

"Derek!"

Mehitabel is a bit breathless and flushed when she comes up to him, wearing her yellow poncho over her clothes, her hair already curling from the humidity. "Sorry I'm late," she says. "We got lost."

"S'okay," Derek says. "I'm glad you made it."

They start moving with the crowds headed toward the elevator that will take them below the falls and then to the walkway leading to the Hurricane Deck. When they get to the door, he turns to her and says, "Ready?" and she nods, and they go through.

For the first few minutes, they don't say much, and Mehitabel focuses on keeping her footing on the wet boards of the walkway.

"See that up there?" Derek says pointing toward a dramatic foaming gush toward the top of the falls. "That's called the Bridal Veil."

They stop to look at it, allowing a family group to go past them, then Mehitabel says, "I'm really sorry for your loss. I just wanted to say that in person. How are you—holding up?"

"Some days are hard." He gazes at the waterfall, a small smile on his face. "I miss her."

"I wish—" she stops. What does she wish? She doesn't trust herself to speak.

Derek nods, briefly touches her forearm with a fingertip. He says, "Let's keep going. We're not at the Hurricane Deck yet."

"Am I gonna get wet?" Mehitabel asks.

Derek chuckles. "I hope you brought a change of clothes." Then he turns and walks off.

Mehitabel hurries after him. It was a good thing she'd decided at the last minute to face this moment on her own because Jawari, like a cat, hates getting wet.

As she and Derek climb toward the falls, Mehitabel's main impression is the tremendous force of the sound. The power of the water. She's never seen anything like this, even in Switzerland where she and Kiki had visited Foroglio Falls near Locarno.

When she gets to the Hurricane Deck, Derek is waiting for her, and he has to shout over the roar of the water, "Hold on to the rail!" He takes her arm and gently pulls her toward him to stand at the railing. A maelstrom of water and wind takes her breath away and her first thought is *why bother with these stupid ponchos?* because she is immediately soaked through to the skin.

"Turn around!" Derek shouts and points upward. "Bridal Veil!"

They stand there, letting the force of the water and wind pound them, and, at one point, Mehitabel reaches for Derek's hand because it feels like she's about to be swept away. His hand is warm and strong, and he holds her steady. He's smiling.

Epilogue

"Those are *perfect* for you," the clerk says in accented English.

This little jewelry store is on a side street near the Church of the Assumption. The earrings have pear-shaped diamonds surrounded by green amethysts. They drop from square-cut diamond clips centered in carved, white gold.

"Magnificent with that hair color," the clerk says, her tone simultaneously unctuous and insincere.

"I don't know," the woman says, turning her head first one way, then the other to see all angles of her reflection. "They might be a bit...much." She pulls the earrings off and places them carelessly on the counter, then peers into the tray of sparkling baubles the clerk has laid out.

The woman plucks another pair from the tray, this one with yellow diamonds set in platinum. Simple drops. Less dramatic. She puts them on, considers her reflection.

"Very nice choice," the clerk says and the woman smiles.

The door to the shop opens and another customer enters. The man, in pristine white pants and pale blue sweater, dark chest hair visible above the deep V, greets the clerk in Greek, and the clerk turns and says to the woman, "Excuse me, please," and moves off to help the man who, it seems, is interested in her selection of Rolex watches.

The woman pulls the yellow diamond earrings off her ears and places them back in the tray. She sighs, then turns to the clerk and says, "I have to think about it" and wiggling her fingers in the air as a goodbye, walks out of the shop, the bell over the door tinkling lightly as the door closes.

In the street, the woman walks slowly away from the jewelry shop, her hand in her jacket pocket, her fingers inside the left pocket curling around the earring nestled inside.

Acknowledgments

I wrote this book during the Pandemic year of 2020, wanting to say something about resilience and forgiveness and created families. In that spirit, I want to thank the created family of readers and supporters who rallied around this book and helped it become what it is.

Innumerable thanks to my partner Betsy Carson for bringing her sharp eye for detail and character to my process. Her no bullshit feedback kept me honest every step of the way, and her unflagging encouragement kept me writing, especially when I wanted to quit.

Thank you to Joan Adler, friend of my heart, sister from another mother and my number one fan. You are my characters' greatest champion. Every writer should have such a dedicated and passionate reader in their lives.

Thank you to my other wonderful and generous readers for their feedback and encouragement: Danielle Winston, Kyna Morgan, Jen Dupree, Leah Gage, Pia Owens, Jill Harrigan and Philip Clark.

Thank you to Jennifer Caven for bringing discernment and expertise to the proofreading process.

About the Author

Kate Kaminski is a writer and an award-winning indie filmmaker. Her four feature films, "(I'm Living) a Charmed Life," "The Barghest," "Trip" and "The Crew," are distributed internationally by Gemini Entertainment. She has a master's degree in film production from Boston University and has taught fiction writing, screenwriting, filmmaking and film studies. She and her partner live and make films in southern Maine.

www.ingramcontent.com/pod-product-compliance
Lightning Source LLC
Chambersburg PA
CBHW060327310726
48976CB00007B/2473